NO ONE HAS TO KNOW: A SECRET WORTH KEEPING

BY: SHANICE B.

No One Has To Know: A Secret Worth Keeping

Copyright © 2018 Shanice B.

ISBN: 9781720298274

TO KEEP UP WITH MY LATEST RELEASES PLEASE SIGN UP TO MY MAILING LIST BY VISITING MY WEBSITE BELOW...

www.shaniceb.com

BOOKS BY SHANICE B.

LOVE ME IF YOU CAN (1-3)

WHO'S BETWEEN THE SHEETS: MARRIED TO A CHEATER

(1-4)

LOVING MY MR WRONG: A STREET LOVE AFFAIR (1-2)

A LOVE SO DEEP: NOBODY ELSE ABOVE YOU (SPIN-OFF TO

WHO'S BETWEEN THE SHEETS)

STACKING IT DEEP: MARRIED TO MY PAPER

(STANDALONE)

KISS ME WHERE IT HURTS (1-3)

HE LOVES THE SAVAGE IN ME: A TWISTED LOVE AFFAIR

(1-2)

LOVE, I THOUGHT YOU HAD MY BACK (STANDALONE)

MARRIED TO A DEKALB COUNTY BULLY (STANDALONE)

ALL I EVER WANTED WAS YOU: A TWISTED LOVE STORY

(1-2)

FEENIN' FOR THAT DOPE DICK (AN EROTIC SHORT STORY)

I KNOW THEY SAID THE FIRST LOVE IS THE SWEETEST, BUT THAT FIRST CUT IS THE DEEPEST. I TRIED TO KEEP US TOGETHER, BUT YOU WAS TO BUSY KEEPING SECRETS. _DRAKE

SYNOPSIS

"Sometimes when you think you know a person, that's when you learn that you never knew them at all."

Layla and her brother Lamar have always been close, but their relationship soon starts to become rocky when Layla leaves her abusive boyfriend and moves in with Lamar and his girlfriend Promise. Lamar believes he's doing the right thing by stepping in and helping his baby sister, but he soon will see that he has made a fatal mistake.

When Promise learns that her boyfriend Lamar has cheated on her, Promise feels as if her perfect world has been shattered right before her eyes.

As she tries to mend her broken heart, she soon realizes that this will not be an easy task because she can't let go of the pain of her man hurting her.

Promise and Layla are both having a hard time coping with their love lives. They both feel as if they don't have anyone in their corner to help them get through their difficult time. When they realize that they're all each other have, that's when an unlikely friendship begins to bloom that is unbreakable.

It only takes one night of too many drinks, before their close friendship turns into a hot steamy love affair.

They both know if Lamar ever finds out about their secret all hell will break loose, but they will soon come to the conclusion, that what Lamar don't know can't hurt him. Will Promise and Layla be able to keep their love a secret or will Lamar recognize the red flags that something just isn't right?

PROLOGUE

"Lay down babygirl, let me take care of you," Layla whispered into my ear.

This was something that she always said to me when she about to tongue me down. I was getting accustomed to her licking my pussy whenever my man was nowhere to be found.

As I laid down on the same bed that I shared with my boyfriend of two years I knew what we were doing was wrong, but in my mind, I gave zero fucks because it wasn't like he had been loyal to me these past two years that we had been together.

As her lips met my own, my heart skipped a beat, and my juice box began to drip with anticipation.

When she slid up my mini yellow sundress, thoughts of my man quickly were pushed to the back of my mind. All I wanted to do was get my pussy ate without thinking about any of the consequences that was sure to follow if my man found out.

"You just don't know how much I want you to be mine, you have no clue how I lay in bed every night and wish that you would leave him," Layla whispered into my ear before flicking her tongue against my earlobe.

I moaned as she began to caress my kitty kat with her hand while she placed feather light kisses on my neck.

I knew without a doubt that Layla cared for me and worshipped the fucking ground I walked on, but I also knew that no matter what, we could never be together. My man would kill us both if he found out what we were doing behind his back.

"You like that?" Layla asked me.

I stared into her pretty brown hazel eyes as I nodded my head at her question. There was no way in hell I was trusting myself to speak.

As she pulled my sundress straps off my shoulders, I began to whimper as she flicked her wet tongue over each of my pierced nipples.

After she had shown each of my nipples some attention she quickly slid her tongue into my mouth and began to kiss me with so much passion that my whole body grew weak. I could feel her tongue ring dancing in my mouth as her tongue played with my own.

A few moments later she pulled away from me and quickly slid between my chocolate colored thighs. My whole body began to tremble as she flicked her tongue against my clit just before she slid a finger gently into my tight little honey box.

I squeezed my eyes shut as I began to grind my pussy against her finger as she continued to make love to my clit. It had been so long since my kitty had been licked or even fucked by my nigga. My sex life wasn't hitting on shit when it came to my man fucking me, I was always eager to cum, and she was just as eager to make me.

"Shit," I cried.

Layla stared seductively at me as she slid her finger out my little coochie and licked them clean.

When Layla was done, she then pushed my legs farther apart as she began to lick her hungry tongue inside my pussy hole. I gripped the bed sheets with my right hand as I whimpered for her to not stop. When she started back fingering me, I began to cry out in pleasure because I was on the verge of cuming.

I began to whine as she slid a second finger into my honey pot all while sucking on my clit and slurping my juices.

"I'm about to cum," I choked out.

I cried out her name and gripped both sides of the bed as I filled her hungry mouth with my cream.

Layla didn't move until she had drained every little drop of cum that was left. She pulled away from me a few seconds later before placing soft kisses on my shaved honey box.

I rubbed my hands through her long black dreads before she lifted her head up and her eyes met my own.

"I'm nowhere done pleasing you," Layla said to me before she kissed me in the mouth.

We pulled away from one another for only a few moments and that's when Layla took my place on the bed.

"Come here babygirl, come ride my face for a little while."

I didn't hesitate to get into position to sit on top of her face while she ate my cookie. Her tongue inside my pussy had me about to lose my damn mind. It was feeling just that fucking good. As I rocked back and forth Layla kept a firm grip on my hips as she continued to make love to me with her mouth.

When she was done tasting me, she quickly smacked me on my ass, and slid me off of her.

"Get on your hands and knees," Layla instructed me.

I did as I was told and nearly passed out when she began to place kisses on my ass just before she flicked her tongue inside my ass crack. I moaned loudly when I felt her hands slide between my thighs. As her finger toyed with my clit, she continued to lick her tongue around my booty hole.

"I'm about to cum," I choke out with ecstasy.

Layla didn't have any plans of stopping, she was set out to make me cum as much as she could, and it wasn't long before my kitty kat began to drip with white cream.

Layla gladly slid her finger into my creamy love nest just so she could get a taste of me. My legs were shaking and sweat was dripping from my body like I had ran a fucking marathon. After Layla had licked me clean for the last time, she quickly squeezed my ass before pulling me by my long black hair.

She was just about to say something to me when I heard my front door slam shut. I knew then that my man had just made it home.

"Fuck," I hissed as I hurried to get off the bed.

Layla began getting the room in order while I dashed towards the other side of the room to get myself back together.

I made sure to put my yellow sundress on correctly and took a look at myself just to make sure I didn't look like I had just gotten fucked.

I was grateful when I turned back towards Layla to find that she had fixed the bed and had hid the scent of sex by spraying some air freshener in the air. I walked over to where she was posted up by my window and placed a kiss on her soft pink lips.

"Promise, Layla where the fuck ya'll at!" Lamar yelled out from downstairs.

"We upstairs!" We both shouted back at him.

I could tell by the way that he sounded that something was wrong. Lamar was pissed but neither Layla and I knew why.

Layla quickly lit her a cigarette, which was something she always did when she was nervous or stressed about some shit.

I was just about to speak, but Layla quickly placed her index finger over my lips.

"Baby lets remain calm. I got you. You should know I wouldn't ever do anything to jeopardize what you have with my brother. What you and I do when he ain't around is our little secret, no one has to know."

I nodded my head at her.

The worry that I must have had on my face earlier was wiped cleaned off after hearing Layla promising me that no matter what happened our secret was going to stay safe.

Even though I felt somewhat guilty about cheating on my man with his sister, it wasn't enough that I wanted to ever leave Layla alone.

If Lamar would have been taking care of me sexually instead of cheating on me there would have been no way that Layla could have slid her way into my life, I told myself. But as I stared over at her and noticed just how beautiful this girl was, I had to really rethink that shit.

Never in my life had I ever been with a female. But the way Layla was fucking on me, I was beginning to rethink my sexuality.

I looked up towards the clock and noticed that it is was one in the afternoon. Red flags began to go off in my head.

"Why is Lamar home in the first place?" Layla asked me curiously.

I shook my head because I had no answer to her question.

When he stepped through the door Layla and I both gasped as he aimed his pistol at us both.

"You thought I wouldn't find out about ya'll little secret. You thought I was too dumb to figure out my baby sister was fucking my damn girl." Lamar snarled at Layla.

Layla and I both tried to speak at the same time, but Lamar wasn't trying to hear any of the shit that we were saying.

"How the fuck could ya'll both betray me like this?" he asked in a shaky voice.

"Please Lamar put the gun down and let us talk about this shit," Layla tried to reason with him.

"Shut the fuck up Layla. Bitch you my fucking sister, I took your ass in when that piece of shit of a boyfriend was beating your ass, you fucked up when you betrayed me hoe," he spat violently.

"Let me explain," I told Lamar with tears in my eyes.

"What do you need to explain bitch? I work all fucking day to keep a roof over your fucking head and this how you going to do a nigga? I know I fucked up by cheating on you, but I never thought you would do some shit like this. I have gone over and beyond to make your ass happy and you have the audacity to do some fucked up shit like this to me. I was the one who brought your weak ass your own clothing store that you claimed you had to have. The lights barely stay on in that bitch, but the doors still open because I'm the one who make sure that it stays that way. I'm the one who paying all the fucking bills in this damn house and making sure you still driving the latest whip. Bitch you need to bow down at my fucking feet and be thanking my ass, but what do you do?

You rather go behind my back and fuck my damn baby sister. Shid, I didn't even know either one of you even swung that way!" he shouted.

When Lamar took his pistol off safety I knew shit was about to get real.

Layla grabbed my hand as the tears fell from both of our eyes.

Lamar wasn't looking like himself, he looked so fucking twisted in the face, his eyes were bloodshot red like he was high on some type of drug. I saw nothing but evil when I looked at him and I could tell that he wanted us both dead.

"Please," I heard myself beg.

"Don't beg now bitch!" Lamar shouted before pulling the trigger.

CHAPTER 1

PROMISE

THREE MONTHS EARLIER...

I always thought that I had this perfect relationship, you know the one that Bey and Jay always shown to the media. Well that's what I thought I had with Lamar until reality slapped my naïve ass in the face. There wasn't no such thing as a perfect relationship and I learned that shit the hard way. Growing up I always dreamed of marrying the man of my dreams and having all his babies, but as I became older I realized that there was no such thing as prince charming, he didn't exist in today's word. I had to accept the fact that this was a reality and not a damn fairytale.

I guess, if I wanted to place the blame on anyone I would say it was my mother's fault. I didn't know my daddy and she didn't know him either. I believe this was why I craved a relationship with a man who would give me the world. I wanted a man who would love and cherish me and give me his all. I craved a love so deep that even the ocean would be jealous of it.

My mother raised me to be independent and to never depend on a nigga for shit, but as I stared at my reflection in the mirror I felt ashamed because I had done the complete opposite of what my mother always preached for me to do.

I was only eighteen years old when my mother was killed by a drunk driver. To this day it still hurt me to my heart because I never got the chance to tell her just how much I loved her. I regretted not being close to the woman who had given birth to me. I needed her more than ever, but she was gone, and I was all alone.

As the tears fell from my eyes I quickly wiped them away. There was no way I was about to cry over a nigga. Hell nall, my mama didn't raise no weak bitch, she didn't play that shit. She raised me to be tough and to never let a nigga run over my ass. As I sat back and reminisced about my childhood, now I understood why she raised me with an iron fist. She didn't want me to end up like her.

Mom, I wish you were still here, I know you would know what to do about this shit I have found myself in, I said to myself.

Now that I was grown and had a relationship of my own, I understood what my mother meant when she told me to watch who I laid down with because sometimes you could be laying down with the devil.

Just remembering her saying that shit brought me back to Lamar and what I thought we had.

When Lamar walked into my life two years ago, I was twenty-two years old and was attending Middle Georgia State University (Warner Robins Campus) for Business Administration. I had a part-time job waiting tables at night at Steak and Shake just so I could make ends meet. Lamar came into the restaurant one night and took a seat as he waited for me to take his order. He had to wait for a good minute before I could even get to him because we were extremely short staffed that particular night.

Most customers would have gotten irritated with having to wait for service, but Lamar was very understandable and patient. When our eyes locked on each other I fell in love with him on sight. The chemistry was intense, and I didn't understand it at first.

As the months began to fly by, I found myself wondering if I was falling in love to fast and wondering if we were even on the same page. I mean just because you had a deep attraction to someone doesn't mean that they felt the same back in return. But Lamar put my mind at ease when he told me that our love was equal.

Lamar was every bitch's fantasy. He's twenty-eight years old, about 6'2, light skinned, with pretty brown hazel eyes. He rocked a low cut with his sides faded with a nice thick beard to match. The nigga was sexy as hell and he knew that shit, I guess that could explain why he found it hard to keep his dick inside his pants. He claimed he loved me, but ain't that what a lot of niggas tell their girls these days?

I hated that I was so blinded by Lamar's charisma and his good dick that I was clueless about who he truly was. I never questioned anything that he told me, and I found myself believing everything that came out his mouth until I learned that his ass was a big liar.

One thing I hated the most was a liar, the second thing I hated was a nigga who cheated on his girl. Lamar had done both to me which put his ass on my *YOU AIN'T SHIT LIST*.

I was still devastated about him cheating on me late last year with one of his ex-girlfriends from college. I was still hurt about the shit because I never saw it coming.

When we first met, Lamar was straight up with me about his ex. He told me that they met in college and they had dated for about three years, but they broke up after she lost their baby. The whole time that Lamar was explaining this to me he also was reassuring me that him and his ex were over each other and he was ready to give me his heart.

My dumb ass hung on his every word and trusted him. Big mistake on my part, I was dumb for trusting his ass. His ex-girlfriend eventually moved back to town and that's when shit went to hell and back.

Back then Lamar and I weren't living together but we were making plans to.

I didn't ever suspect Lamar of cheating on me until I noticed that his phone was always buzzing all throughout the day. He lied and told me it was work related, but I was far from stupid, I knew no job was going to be buzzing their employee at eleven at night.

I eventually found out about him and the bitch one night when he was asleep next to me. His phone kept buzzing so me being the nosy bitch that I was, I grabbed it and picked up, that's when I learned the fucking truth. The bitch was singing like a fucking bird and gave me some very interesting details about her and Lamar's fuck sections that they had after he got off work.

I confronted him and threatened to leave his ass if he didn't cut that bitch off. He cried and begged me to stay, but I wasn't hearing any of that shit at first. Eventually, I caved in because one thing about Lamar when he wanted something he could be very persistent and well he wanted me back and he eventually won me back by buying me my own clothing store where I sold hang bags, lingerie, perfumes, and different types of name brand clothes at a discounted price. I always dreamed of owning my own store, he made that dream come true, and this was the only reason I decided to get back with him.

My clothing store had just opened up a few months ago and things were moving rather slowly at the moment, but I knew eventually my business was going to get the recognition that it deserved.

Right now, Lamar was the breadwinner and had just opened his own loan company called Lamar's loan services about four months ago. He had gotten most of his experience from working at First Franklin as an account manager for over three years, but he soon decided owning his own company would be the best option for his future. His dream was to start his own loan company and he had done just that.

The money that he was now making had us living in a three-bedroom home, with two bathrooms, a two-door garage, and a built-in swimming pool in the back. I'm not going to lie we were living good and we were blessed to not be struggling, but nothing is ever perfect because life wasn't meant to be easy or perfect.

Now that Lamar was running his own company he was rarely ever home. This was beginning to put a strand on our relationship. I was still trying to heal from him cheating on me and now that he was working longer hours I was beginning to have them awful thoughts that maybe he had found someone else.

Lamar and I had been through a lot of ups and downs in our relationship, but never did he ever go days or even over a week without fucking me. Lamar was the type of nigga who wanted to fuck at least twice a day, but now it was to the point where this nigga didn't even have the time to let me suck his dick.

My mother didn't raise no damn fool. I knew if he could cheat on me one time he could do it again if the opportunity presented itself. Even though he claimed he would never break my heart again, I still didn't trust his ass. I was frustrated because I had given this nigga two years of my life and there was no way in hell I was about to let him make a fool of me a second time.

Just as the crazy thoughts began to enter my mind that's when I heard Lamar's booming voice downstairs.

"Promise," I'm home he called out.

"I'm coming!" I yelled out.

I hurried to finish brushing the tangles out my long weave before I placed my hair into a high ponytail and headed downstairs.

"Baby, what you been doing all day?" Lamar asked as he walked over to where I was standing.

"I was at the shop most part of the day," I told him just before I stared up into his hazel brown eyes.

When he placed his hands over my cheek and kissed me gently on my lips my body reacted even when I didn't want it to. Even though, I was frustrated and suspicious of everything that Lamar did or said I still couldn't take the love away that I felt for him.

"Baby, I know I've been neglecting you lately, but I'm just doing whatever I can to make you happy and keep you living good. We wouldn't have any of this shit if I didn't run my company. I just want you to know that I love you," he whispered into my ear before embracing me in a hug.

I was the first one who pulled away from the embrace and that's when he looked at me with confusion in his eyes.

"What's wrong baby? I can tell something is bothering you."

I took a few steps back because I felt as if I couldn't breath and my thoughts were becoming scrambled.

I bit down on my bottom lip but didn't have the nerve to face him.

"Promise, what the hell is up with you?" Lamar asked with even more concern.

I was near tears but there was no way I was going to let them fall.

"Nothing is wrong," I muttered before turning away from him and heading towards the kitchen so I could get dinner started. I was just about to open the fridge when Lamar grabbed me by my arm.

"I've been with you long enough to know when something is bothering you, I'm not going to leave you alone until you tell me."

I could tell how he was looking that he was being dead ass serious so that's when I made the decision to let him know exactly how I truly felt.

"I'm just frustrated and tired of us not being able to get this shit right."

"What the fuck are you talking about?" Lamar asked with a muddled look on his face.

"Since you have opened your own loan company you rarely ever home and when you do come home all you do is eat, shower, and go to bed. We spend no time together, we don't go out, and none of my needs are being met. You not even fucking me, a bitch has needs. And just like you claim you know me, well I know you just as well. I know for a fact that you the type of nigga who likes to fuck at least twice a day. We not fucking at all, I ain't even sucking your dick in the mornings, so what I'm wondering is, who are you fucking because it damn sure isn't me?" I asked bluntly.

The fact that Lamar pressed me for the truth was the only reason why I decided to give it to him raw and uncut. He wanted to know what was wrong and now he knew.

Lamar looked at me like he was shocked and wasn't expecting me to say any of the shit that I had just left my mouth.

"Baby, I'm working my ass off to provide for us, I'm not fucking around with anyone."

I rolled my eyes at him as the anger and resentment began to boil over.

"Don't stand there and fucking lie to me. Last time you told me you weren't cheating you were lying through your teeth."

"Will you please just let that shit go, I'm not cheating on you. Yes, I fucked up and cheated on you the first time with my ex, but I'm not on that bullshit now, you all I fucking want why don't you trust me!" he yelled at me.

The fact that this nigga thought it was okay to raise his voice at me was what really set me off.

"I don't trust you because all you do is cheat and lie, you would still be fucking that bitch if I would have never found out. I have every right to question everything you do!" I shouted before I grabbed a plate from off the counter and threw it at his ass.

Lamar moved out the way as dishes started flying at him.

"You don't make time for a bitch no more, you don't fuck a bitch no more, so why in the hell are we together!" I cried out to him.

I was just about to throw my last plate when he pushed me up against the wall and placed my hands over my head.

"Stop this shit Promise, ain't nobody cheating on you or even trying to cheat on you. I'm sorry if I ain't been giving you what you need, but I promise I'm going to do better, just calm the fuck down."

I tried pushing him off me, but Lamar wasn't having the shit.

"I'm working so much only because I'm trying to get everything situated. I have so many clients that are coming in and I'm having to log in information and make sure that everything is squared away. Right now, I only have two females that are working for me so its limited in what we can do. I'm going back and double checking all the accounts and constantly praying that the software I'm using will hold up until next year. I'm seriously thinking about hiring an assistant accountant to help me work on some of the older loan accounts that were taken out when I first opened up a few months ago. If I hire an assistant accountant I won't have to work so many hours. The two women that I have already hired only know how to do so much, so I need someone with more experience."

I shook my head the whole time as he tried to explain himself, but I still didn't know what to fucking believe.

"Get the fuck off of me Lamar, I'm sick of this shit. Just be a man and tell me the fuckin truth."

"Promise I can't help the fact that I'm working long hours. I rather be here fucking on you then there all day trying to log data into the system and make sure the books are up to date."

I was near tears, but Lamar wouldn't let me go.

When he placed his lips on mine, he kissed me roughly at first before pulling away from me.

"You say you want some dick so I'm going to give your ass exactly what you been asking for."

I gasped when he roughly pushed up my red mini dress and pulled my black thong down my legs. He picked me up and roughly slid his long tongue into my mouth. I couldn't resist him even if I wanted to. My pussy was throbbing, and I haven't been fucked in almost three weeks.

I moaned loudly as he carried me up the long flight of stairs and pushed me down on our king-sized bed. I licked my lips as he slid down his khaki pants and pulled off his royal blue t-shirt (which was his preferred dress code for work).

When he was completely naked he stared down at me before he told me to get down on my knees and suck his dick.

I didn't hesitate to slide him into my hungry mouth. His monster rod throbbed in my mouth as I sucked and slurped on his love stick. When he gripped my hair with his hand I already knew he was about to get ready to do some damage.

"Yes baby, just like that, suck on this dick like you can't live without it," Lamar muttered.

My throat began to burn as he deep throated me. I gagged and almost felt as if I was about to throw up, but there was no way I was about to back down from pleasing my man.

I opened my eyes and stared up at him as I continued to please him. My throat was sore as hell when he finally pulled his tool from my wet mouth.

I had sucked my man to perfection, his love stick was covered in slob, and was ready to be inserted into my tight little honey pot. My kitty kat began to clinch just thinking about him filling my walls up.

My heart began to race as he slid between my legs and began to please me with his tongue. I cried out his name as he slid a finger into my treasure box as he sucked on my clit. I closed my eyes and began to rock my body back and forth as he continued to please me.

"I'm about to cum," I choked out.

I screamed out his name as he started to slide his tongue in and out of my honey box. A few moments later my whole body grew weak as I filled Lamar's mouth with my cream.

He licked my kitty clean before he finally came up for air.

"Fuck," I managed to whisper as he trailed wet kisses up and down my body.

I moaned his name loudly as he sucked on my neck.

"Are you ready for this dick?" he whispered into my ear.

He didn't even give me a chance to respond before he pushed my thighs apart and slid his anaconda into my love tunnel. He pushed my hair from out my face as he placed his lips on mine. Our bodies were finally at one and I felt as if I was where I wanted to be. He was filling my little coochie up and I was loving every second of it.

"Damn, you feel so damn good," Lamar kept muttering in my ear as he deep stroked me.

I felt as if I was on some type of drug, my juice box was wetter than an ocean and his love stick was hitting all the right spots. I gasped when he slid my legs over his shoulder and began to pound my kitty.

"I'm about to cum baby," I screamed out as he started to slam into me more deeply.

There was no way I was able to hold in this massive explosion that I was feeling inside. As I milked his love stick with my cream, he slammed into me one last time before he spilled his seed inside my sugar walls.

Both of our bodies were weak from the lovemaking that had just gone down. I smelled nothing but sex in our bedroom, as the cool air from the ceiling fan hit my naked body. I was just about to slide out of bed to head to the bathroom, but that's when Lamar pulled me closer to him.

"Don't leave baby," he said gently to me.

Instead of showering I laid back down in Lamar's arm. As he caressed my bare skin he placed gentle kisses on my neck and cheek.

"Baby, I know you feel that I'm never hardly home, but I promise you that I'm not on no fuck shit. I learned my lesson the first time. My life wouldn't have any purpose if you left me."

A single tear fell from my eyes and he quickly brushed it away.

"You have my heart forever and always baby, I love you. Just let me get this shit straight with my company and I promise you will have me all to yourself. Just be patient with me."

I nodded my head and told him that I understood.

A few moments later that's when I heard him gently snoring next to me. I turned over and sure enough Lamar had fell to sleep. I gently moved his arm off of my body and slid off the bed. I tiptoed towards the bathroom and closed the door gently behind myself being careful not to wake him.

As I stared at myself in the mirror I finally felt some type of relief that soon things between Lamar and I was going to get better. As soon as he got things right at work our relationship was going to become stronger than ever. I only prayed that he was telling me the truth.

CHAPTER 2

LAMAR

I know I had fucked up by cheating on Promise and I was doing everything in my power to try to make things right, but I felt none of that shit was being recognized by her. She didn't trust my ass and that what hurt me the most. I just wished that she could forget what I had done, but I knew that wasn't going to happen anytime soon.

Cheating on her was the wrong thing to damn do, and now I was going to have to live with the consequences. If I could go back and turn things around I damn sure would, I would have never let my past walk back into my life and turn it upside down.

I rubbed the sleep from my eyes as my phone began to blast **Travis Scott-***Serenade*.

It was time for my ass to get up and get ready for work. I dreaded getting out of bed, but I knew the company would fall under if I sat my ass home. I glanced over at Promise and notice she was still sleeping like a baby. I placed a kiss on her forehead before I hurried towards the bathroom and closed the door behind me. I brushed my teeth until my breath was fresh, after I was done I turned on the shower, and adjusted the water to a decent temperature.

I stepped into the shower a few moments later so I could take care of my hygiene before I headed to work. As the steamy hot water began to pound down on my tired body I began to wonder where Promise and I were going to be in the next five years. If shit didn't get better, then this I highly doubted that she was going to be with my ass. A nigga was stressing bad because I had a lot of shit that was on my plate with no help.

Here I was at the age of twenty-eight and was doing all I could to make my girl happy as well as myself. I was paying all the bills by myself due to the fact Promise store wasn't hardly bringing in enough profit, I wasn't complaining about the shit because I was willing to do anything to keep a smile on my girl's face, but when the issues with the relationship started to come into play that's when I started stressing.

When I first met Promise two years ago everything was perfect, and I was extremely happy, but I fucked all that up due to temptation and not really closing the door to my past. My heart felt heavy every time I thought about Amber and the love we once had. I met Amber when I was attending Middle Georgia State University (Warner Robins Campus) and fell in love with her instantly. She was beautiful in every way. Amber was white Italian and came from a family who had a shit load of money, she was medium in height, beautiful long dark hair, with pretty green eyes that you could lost in.

I could tell she was totally different from the other women that I had fucked around with before her. She was smart as hell, funny, and we had so much shit in common. We were both majoring in Accounting and the love of numbers was what really brought us together. Her dream was to one day own her accounting firm, but after she learned she was pregnant with my baby that was when our fairytale romance went to hell and back.

I'm not going to say she started hating me, but I could tell things started to change very quickly with us. The tension was undeniable, and

I could tell getting pregnant by a black man wasn't in her plans. Not once did she ever tell me how she felt about being pregnant, but her actions spoke volumes and the vibe I got from her was something I could never forget. I knew in my heart that getting her pregnant was something she wasn't expecting, and it had thrown her for a curve ball. The glow that she once had when we first met was no longer there.

Not once did I ever want her to drop out of school or stop her dream of owning her own accounting firm. All I truly wanted was her to continue school and have the baby, if that meant sitting out for a semester or two then I was ready to do what I could to help her. Just when I thought everything was going to be okay that's when I learned that she had gone behind my back and aborted our baby. To this day that shit still hurt me to my fucking heart that the one girl who I had fallen in love with had aborted my seed.

A single tear fell down my cheek as I thought back to that day when she finally told me that she had aborted our child. I lost it for a minute and I instantly remembered grabbing her by the throat and squeezing as hard as I could. I finally snapped out of the trance that I had been in when I noticed she was turning bright red and could barely breath. I let her go only to push her down on the floor. I walked out of her dorm that particular day and never looked back at her. I avoided her at all costs, so many times she tried reaching out to me, but never did I ever respond. She was the first bitch who ever broke my heart, I had given her three years of my life only to find out that she was a baby killer.

The next following year we both graduated from Accounting and went our separate ways. I never saw her ass again and that was just fine with me. I moved on with my life and she did the same as well.

When Promise came into my life I was still hurt over what Amber had done, but I wanted to give Promise my heart regardless of the pain that I was feeling inside. I fell in love with Promise on sight and did whatever I could to let her know that she was the only woman in my life. Never did I ever expect to bump into Amber ever again, but that's exactly what eventually happened. I just happened to meet her at a work conference and that's when the past came rushing back to me stronger than ever.

When Amber came back into my life that's when I learned that the love that we shared some years earlier was far from dead. After her and I both sat down with a cup of coffee we both talked about our past and the lost of our baby. I could tell that Amber was nervous as hell as she spoke to me, but when she noticed that I didn't have the hate in my heart for her any longer, she quickly began to relax as she told me the true reason why she aborted our child.

When she told me that she would have been disowned and cut off financially if she would have kept our baby, I finally began to realize the situation that she was in when we were in college. There was no way her family was going to go along with her getting pregnant without being married first, they would have gone into a rage and have cut her off for good. There was no way Amber wanted to lose her education or her family for falling pregnant by me. After we talked and cried about the decision that was made that's when one thing led to another.

For three months I continued to smash Amber without Promise knowing anything, but shit started getting very crazy and intense when Amber decided to move back to Warner Robins to open up her own accounting firm. When the phone calls and text messages started to become too frequent that's when Promise began to get a feeling that something was going on, but me being the type of nigga that I was, I played the shit smooth as ever.

But we all know what is done in the dark will always come to the light, so when Promise found out about Amber the indecision of not knowing to stay with Promise or make things work with my first love was instantly made for me. Just thinking about Promise leaving me really put a sour taste in my life. There was no way I wanted Promise to walk out on me because I knew that no matter what Promise loved a nigga and she would never hurt me.

What Amber and I had was special, but Promise was the one I couldn't live without, so I chose her over Amber which really broke Amber's heart, but I felt like Amber had already had her chance which she had already fucked that up years earlier.

We all made decisions in life and Amber had made hers when she chose her family over our baby. Now it was time for both of us to live with what direction our life was going in. Even though Amber and I would probably never get back together she was always going to have a place in my heart because she was my first love, but she was also the first bitch who shattered it.

I quickly snapped out of the memories of the past when I heard *Travis Scott* blasting *Way Back*. This was my second alarm letting me know that it was soon going to be time for me to head to work. I quickly cut the hot water off and stepped out the shower just before I wrapped a towel around my slim waist.

As soon as I headed back into my bedroom I noticed that Promise was up.

"Good morning beautiful," I said sweetly as I walked over to my closet and began to find me something to wear for that day.

I had about thirty minutes to get dressed and head out the door, there was no way I wanted to be late.

"Good morning," Promise mumbled back.

I knew instantly something was bothering her. As I began to get dressed I tried talking to her, but Promise didn't seem like talking, in fact she ignored my ass. After I had gotten dressed I grabbed my phone and slid it into my pocket.

"What time are you going to be home?" Promise finally asked.

I stopped what I was doing so I could give her my full attention.

"Baby, I don't want to give you a time because I don't want you getting pissed off if I work over."

That was when Promise pushed the covers off her naked body and slid out the bed.

"Yeah, I assume it's going to be after nine right," Promise said with an attitude as she walked past me.

It was too early in the fucking morning to be damn fussing with Promise, so I quickly grabbed her by her arm and told her to cut the bullshit.

She snatched her arm back from me but that didn't stop me from telling her ass how I was feeling at the moment.

"Don't start with me this fucking morning. I'm tired as hell and I'm not in the fucking mood to pacifier you today. We already had this discussion last night about why my hours as so long. Give me time to hire an assistant and you will have more time with me, be fucking patient Promise," I said to her crossly before walking past her.

I looked down at my watch and groaned because fussing with her ass had me running behind. I grabbed my keys off the coffee table and hurried out of the door not even thinking to tell Promise bye.

****

I had been pulling ten-hour shifts lately and a nigga was beyond drained. When lunchtime struck I decided to head next door to subway to get me a sandwich and eat it in my office. My loan company was in the same complex as Subway and Little Caesar pizza. I felt I had picked the perfect location to have my loan company because Little Caesar alone had a lot of traffic coming in and out all throughout the day.

Time I stepped out of my office, the sun hit my face.

Shit it was hot out this fucking door, I said to myself as I headed inside Subway.

It was lunch time so of course I had to wait in line for a good little minute at subway before I was finally able to place my order. I thanked the girl who fixed my sandwich, paid, and headed back towards my office so I could enjoy my lunch in peace.

I quickly slid most of the paperwork that I was filling out aside and logged back into my computer so I could start making preparations to find me a damn assistant. I didn't hesitate to head over to Indeed and post a position for a job for an assistant accountant. After the job was posted I decided to also post it on a few other job sites before finally taking a bite of my steak and cheese sub sandwich.

Soon all of the stress that I was feeling was going to cease to exist I told myself as I ate my lunch.

When my lunch break was over with I quickly started back working on a few of the loan accounts before I heard a knock on my door.

"Mr. Lamar can you come here for a second, I'm having trouble with helping a client."

I pushed my paperwork aside and followed Kasey out of my office and headed towards the front. As we walked down the long hallway I couldn't help but notice Kasey's fat ass jiggling. Kasey was a married woman, but that shit didn't matter these days. She was in her mid-thirties and the bitch was fine as hell. She was chocolate in complexion, with a body that a nigga just couldn't resist. Even though I could feel the sexual chemistry between us both I never once tried the bitch up. There wasn't no bitch on this planet worth losing Promise over. Even though temptation was killing my ass, I wasn't about to go there with Kasey.

Instead of making the shit worse by staring at her curvy figure I quickly looked away. I was relieved when I noticed an older black lady who looked to be in her eighty's sitting down patiently waiting on Kasey to return. After talking with the client for only a few minutes I quickly helped Kasey to update the older lady's information.

I took a seat next to Kasey and showed her exactly where to click so she could update the older lady's information. In the back of my mind I already knew that I had just walked into a trap. Kasey already understood how to update the client's information, she had been working here since I opened my damn company.

After the client had been helped and had left out the office Kasey quickly began to rub her hands against my thigh.

I grabbed her by her hand and moved it away from me.

"Let's keep this shit professional," I told her seriously.

Kasey chuckled before she stood up in her tight white sundress and walked behind me. I tried to get up, but she forced me back down in the chair.

"Where do you think you're going? Don't think I haven't noticed how you been watching me around here. I know you want me, but I want to know what you are going to do about it. If you worried about anyone finding out I promise you I won't say shit if you don't," Kasey chucked into my ear before licking my ear lobe.

"Kasey, will you stop this shit."

I tried to sound irritated, but I was far from it. Just smelling her sweet perfume and her touching on me had a nigga dick begging for attention. I was doing my best to fight the urge of bending her over and giving her exactly what she was asking for.

Instead of entertaining Kasey like I wanted to, I pushed her off me, and quickly headed back to my office.

"What is your fucking problem? Kasey asked.

I turned back towards her and stared into her beautiful brown eyes.

"You my fucking problem, your ass is married, and I have a beautiful bitch waiting for me to come home. I'm not about to give you none of this dick, I don't care what you do. I'm not about to fuck you, Kasey."

She squinted her eyes at me before she started going in on my ass.

"Nigga don't stand here and act like you a faithful ass nigga because no nigga is one hundred percent faithful. What my husband and your girl don't know won't hurt them, now come here and let me suck your dick. I've been wanting to do this since I first started working here."

I closed my eyes because this had to be a fucking dream, there was no way this girl was asking to suck my damn dick. I reopened my eyes a few seconds later and that's when I noticed that this wasn't a dream after all. This was really fucking happening.

Kasey was so close to me that I could feel her breath on my neck.

"I want you, I know that you want to find out what this mouth can do" Kasey whispered into my ear as she began to caress my manhood with her hand.

There was no way in hell I was going to be able to walk away from Kasey offering me head. As Kasey began to kiss on my neck I quickly unzipped my pants and freed my manhood, so she could get to work.

The thought of my girl and what I had promised her instantly was pushed far back in my mind.

Kasey was just too fucking tempting. All I wanted was just a little head, it wasn't like I was going to actually fuck the bitch, I told myself.

When Kasey got into position on her knees I didn't hesitate to slide my dick into her mouth.

"Fuck," I said to myself as she began to work her magic on my pole.

Kasey flicked her tongue over my mushroom head a few times before she slid my thickness into her mouth. I watched her as she swallowed over half of my dick without gagging. Damn, this bitch mouth wasn't no fucking joke, I thought to myself as she sucked and slurped on my tool.

"Shit, Yes, suck this damn dick," I moaned as Kasey continued to deep throat me.

Slob dripped from her mouth and tears fell down her cheeks as I continued to drill my dick into her mouth.

A few moments later she began to jack me with her hand, just before she started to suck on my balls.

"Fuck, I'm about to cum," I choked out.

Instead of Kasey continuing to jack me off she slid my anaconda dick back into her mouth as I shot a load of my semen down her throat.

****

LATER THAT DAY

It wasn't until around eight that night that I finally decided that enough work had been done and it was time for me to head home. Guilt was weighing heavily on my mind, but I brushed it off because it was only just a little head. I didn't even give Kasey the dick and that was what truly counted I told myself.

Kasey had left around five that evening and had acted like nothing between us had happened earlier that day. I was relieved because I wasn't prepared to deal with an obsessive employee. There was no one on this planet that I wanted more than Promise, but sometimes I found myself falling short by cheating on her. I rubbed my hand over my forehead and told myself that I wasn't ever going to let Kasey suck my dick again. Matter fact I was going to try to avoid her ass at all cost and maybe I wouldn't find myself in this situation again.

The office was quiet and dark, as usual I was the only one that stayed behind so I could get all the books and loan accounts in order. There was only one other female that also worked alongside Kasey, but she was on vacation, so Kasey was holding down the front part of the office herself.

After I had locked up the office, I hopped in my car and started on the twenty-minute drive to my home, I couldn't stop thinking about how things had gone down today. I was tempted to fuck Kasey after she had given me that mouth, but I knew if I went there with her there was no going back. I didn't want to do anything that could risk losing what I had at home. I wasn't trying to brag and shit, but I had some good ass wood. I mean it was A1 because I always went over and beyond in pleasing the bitch I was fucking.

If I would have given Kasey a sample of what my dick could do, I promise you I would have had her wanting to leave her husband. Her sucking my dick was the only thing I knew that she could do that wouldn't drive her crazy. I wasn't even the type to eat a bitch's pussy because my head skills were at a level that an average bitch just couldn't handle. I didn't want to make shit hard for myself by giving her any head or dick services.

I pulled up at my crib twenty minutes later and hopped out. I was just about to pull my keys out my pocket, but Promise beat me to it. The door opened, and I quickly walked inside. Promise quietly closed the door behind me as she walked back towards the kitchen to finish cooking. My stomach began to growl as the smell of fried chicken, mac and cheese began to fill the air.

I followed Promise into the kitchen and embraced her in a hug before asking her how her day had been.

"It was okay," Promised muttered before she started flipping the chicken over.

I sighed with frustration because I already knew that Promise was pissed yet again.

Instead of fussing with her I hurried upstairs so I could shower my sins away from earlier that day.

As the hot water covered my body I couldn't help but think about what I had done with Kasey. I knew if Promise ever found out she would leave my ass without thinking twice. As long as I kept Promise happy and did what I was supposed to do she wouldn't think that I had done some foul shit behind her back.

After I was done showering and had given myself a pep talk I decided the best thing to do was to not put myself in situations that I would be tempted to cheat.

After I had dried my body off, I hurried to get dress, and headed back downstairs to find Promise standing at the stove stirring the mac and cheese.

"The chicken is about to come up, I hope you hungry."

"You have no idea how hungry I truly am," I said flirtatiously.

Promise stopped what she was doing, turned around, and glanced at me.

I looked at her with nothing but lust in my eyes and that was all Promise had to see.

She smirked at me before she quickly turned back towards the stove and began to pull the chicken up from the grease. After she had turned the stove off I told her to bring her ass towards me. Promise obeyed and never took her eyes off of me as she headed my way.

No words were spoken verbally because our eyes were doing all the talking. I didn't waste any time pulling off her black shorts, or her yellow tank top. Her titties and pussy were exposed and that's when I took the time to cover her nipples with my hungry mouth.

"Shit," Promise moaned as I began to suck and lick and each of her hard erect nipples.

After I had licked and sucked on each of her nipples, I picked her up and placed her on the kitchen table.

As I kissed and sucked on her neck that's when I slid my hands between her thighs and began to caress her kitty kat. She was soaking wet so I already knew she was feening for some dick, but I had something so much better for her ass. As much as she loved getting dick, she loved her some head as well.

I pulled away from her from only a few seconds just before I flicked my tongue over her clit. Her cries were loud and she wasn't holding anything back. I sucked on her pink pearl as I began to finger her. After she had soaked my finger with her juices I decided to slide in a second one.

"Baby, I love you," Promise managed to cry out.

Instead of responding I continued sucking on her pussy. When her body began to shake and she started whining about she was about to cum, I quickly slid my finger out her love tunnel and replaced it with my tongue. I grabbed one of her nipples and squeezed it gently as I slid my tongue in and out her honey box until she reached her peak.

I licked her coochie until she was clean. After I was done she pulled me towards her before sliding her tongue into my mouth.

We kissed and our tongues danced together until my phone started blasting *21 Savage- Bank Account.*

I broke the kiss when I noticed that it was my baby sister calling me.

Promise continued to kiss and suck on my neck as she began to grab on my dick. Every time I gave Promise head she always made sure that she gave me some head back in return. Tonight wasn't going to be any different. As she unzipped my khaki pants and pulled my dick out my boxers, I decide to shoot Layla's a text that I would call her back in ten minutes.

I was in need of a nut and Promise was the only one who I wanted to give that to me.

When Promised pulled her weave into a ponytail I already knew she was about to give me some A1 head. As she sucked and slobbered on my knob I gently told her just how good she was sucking my dick and how she had me ready to bust. Any time Promise sucked my dick I always liked to cheer my baby on just so she knew she was doing a good job. As I pushed her head farther down on my rod she began to gag and even more slob began to cover my dick.

Tears fell from her eyes but that didn't stop Promise from giving me the best head ever. As she deep throated me she didn't forget to caress my balls in the process. I leaned my head back as the sensation filled my whole body.

"Yes baby, suck on this dick," I kept telling her.

I groaned loudly when she pulled my dick out her mouth and stared to show my balls some attention.

As she licked and sucked on each of my balls I started to jack.

It wasn't long before it was time for me to nut.

"Baby you ready for me to bust?"

Promise nodded her head as she opened up her mouth wide.

"Shit," I groaned as I skeeted my cum into her mouth and watched as she swallowed.

After Promise had drained my dick dry I made sure to help her off the floor.

Promise smirked at me before sliding back on her black shorts, and yellow tank top.

"Sit down baby, I'm about to fix your plate." Promise said with a smile on her face.

I slid my dick back into my boxers and zipped my pants up before taking a seat at the kitchen table.

I couldn't take my eyes off of Promise as she worked her way around the kitchen, I bit down on my lip because her ass was looking so damn good and my dick was still on hard. I quickly snapped out my sex trance when Promise asked me if was still going to call to see what my sister wanted.

"I'm going to call her back after we eat to see what she wanted," I said to Promise as she placed my plate in front of me.

"Okay baby," Promise replied before kissing me on my cheek.

After we were done eating, I helped Promise load the dishwasher and clean the kitchen up before I pulled out my phone so I could call my baby sister back.

Her phone rung close to four times before she finally picked up.

I could barely hear her as she cried into the phone.

"Layla? Are you okay?"

I was beginning to panic because I knew something had happened.

Promise must have known the change in my voice because she quickly stopped what she doing and asked me was things okay.

"Bryson hiiiitttt me again," Layla finally managed to choke out.

"What the fuck you mean he hit you?" I shouted into the phone.

I lost it for a quick minute because I was ready to catch a charge at that very moment.

"Where his bitch ass at?" I yelled into the phone.

"He ain't here at the moment," Layla cried.

"Pack your shit up Layla I'm coming to get you."

"No, don't come Lamar, I will just drive over that way."

"I don't want to hear the shit, pack your shit up and be outside. Promise and I are on our way over there to get you."

I didn't even give Layla time to say anything else before I disconnected the call, grabbed the keys, and told Promise we had to go. Promise didn't question me, she already knew how I was about my baby sister. This nigga was going to find his ass six feet deep if he kept laying his hands on my damn sister.

CHAPTER 3

LAYLA

After hanging up the phone with my brother Lamar, I slowly made my way up the stairs to the bedroom that I shared with my boyfriend Bryson. I pulled out a suitcase that I had in my closet and started to pack some clothes that I was going to take with me. Tears fell from my eyes and stung my bruised cheek as I hurried to pack. I only prayed that Bryson didn't come back here when Lamar pulled up because if he did I already knew Lamar wasn't going to show Bryson any mercy.

The relationship between my brother and my boyfriend was bitter like vinegar. My brother hated Bryson with a passion, but the hate towards my boyfriend was justifiable.

Bryson was a drunk and he was abusive as fuck to me. This wasn't the first time that I had called my brother because Bryson had whooped my ass. I had called my brother a few times over the course of this year because Bryson had either beat me or made me feel like I was some scum under his shoe. I could never take Bryson with large doses, so I would always go to my brother to cry on his shoulder until I felt I was ready to come back home.

I was just tired and fed up with all the bullshit. Bryson wasn't pulling his weight and I was drained literally from doing every fucking thing. The fact that not only was he not helping my ass he was also abusing me in the process. It was time for me to go, I just couldn't take this shit any longer.

I had just pulled a fourteen-hour shift, so a bitch was tired and hungry. I wasn't in the mood to come home to a dirty apartment and no food cooked. Bryson normally got off work around two-thirty every fucking day. He had the time to cook and clean because my hours at the hospital was always long. I worked every single day even on the weekends, but Bryson acted as if he didn't give a damn about the hard work that I was putting in. All he seemed to care about was getting drunk and wasting his money on liquor and cigarettes.

For the past year I had been working as an RN at the Houston County Medical Center. Even though the hours were long, I still didn't see myself doing anything else with my life. Caring for people was something that I always wanted to do since I was a little girl. Now at the age of twenty-six, I considered myself successful. I was living in a two-bedroom apartment, in a substantial neighborhood, I was living the American dream, well at least that was what I liked to tell myself.

Even though I was successful in my career my relationship with my boyfriend Bryson was suffering terribly. Deep down the nigga was jealous of my success and I hated that he felt envious of my career.

He was my man, he was supposed to have been my number one fan, but he would rather see my career burn then for me to make more money than him. Never have I ever been materialistic or cared about who the breadwinner was, but I guess it was an issue for Bryson. He always stressed to me that he was the man in this relationship and he was the one who was supposed to have made the most money. Never was I the type of bitch to rub it in his face that I made more than him, but he constantly brought the shit up.

I didn't give a fuck that he was only a manager at the Golden Cup Bowling Alley (which didn't pay much). I still respected him and never made him feel less of a man. The fact that he had his friends in his ear telling him what they would do in his situation didn't make the shit better. I hated all his friends because I knew something that he was too dumb to realize, they all were jealous of him and the type of relationship that we had. I'm sure if they had the opportunity they would have easily taken his spot if they could have.

After I was done packing, I headed into the bathroom just so I could try to cover my face with a little makeup. I knew when Lamar came he was going to want to see what the damage that Bryson had done and I didn't want my face to look too horrible.

I never thought that Bryson could ever hurt me, but as I stared at my reflection in the mirror I knew that this wasn't true. Bryson and I had been together since we were both eighteen years old, the love we once had used to be so strong, but now I was beginning to think that the love we shared no longer existed.

When Bryson and I first met he treated me like a damn Queen I didn't have to worry about anything. We were so much in love that all the teachers and even our parents always said that Bryson and I was one day going to marry. My mother and father adored Bryson and always told me that whatever I did in life Bryson was always going to support me and be there for me every step of the way.

Falling in love my 12th-grade year wasn't something that I ever expected but it happened. Bryson was popular, and his family had a shitload of money just like my family did. We were the perfect couple and our parents basked in our teenage love.

The plan that I had for myself after I graduated high school was to get my certification to be a CNA and work my way up to the top until I became an RN. Bryson dream was to attend college with his football scholarship but after blowing his knee out at his last high school game his whole plan ended up changing. His dream of one-day going pro were slim to none so he decided to go to the local college for Aircraft and landed a job working on the Warner Robins Air Force base.

As I attended my first four years of college to work towards becoming an RN, Bryson was the one who basically was the breadwinner. He was the one who paid all the bills, while I went to school part-time and worked at the nursing home on the weekends.

At first, Bryson was very much supportive just like my parents always told me that he would be. He insisted that I needed to focus on going to school more than working, so working weekends was all he would allow me to do. He always told me he wanted the best for me and I believed him when he told me this.

Even though I wasn't bringing home hardly any money back then, he never once made me feel as if I wasn't pulling my share of the load. I went to school every day, but I also cooked and made sure that our apartment stayed clean, he was satisfied with me just doing that. To me life was perfect until he one day switched up on my ass.

It all started when he got laid off from his job working on base last year. I could understand the stress that he was feeling being that all the bills were on him to pay. By this time I had just gotten certified as an LPN and I told him that I was willing to work fulltime and go to school part-time just so we could make ends meet.

At first, he didn't want to do it, but after the bills started rolling in he decided that was the only option, so we wouldn't lose everything that he had worked so hard to get.

At first things were going well, but I could tell that Bryson hated the situation that we were in. The stress eventually built up and came out one night when he invited his boys to come over to drink with him.

Him and his friends partied until the next morning, after they left he was so drunk that he could barely stand up. Never in my life had I ever seen Bryson that wasted but that time he was. He had a lot of shit on his mind because that's when his true feelings for me came out and that's when the abuse started.

I snapped out of my thoughts when I noticed that my phone was vibrating in my pocket. When I noticed it was Bryson calling I quickly ignored his call. There was nothing that Bryson and I had to talk about. Tonight, was going to be the last time he ever laid his hands on me ever again. When he did bring his ass home later on tonight, he was going to find me gone. There was no way I wanted to live my life in an abusive relationship. I had too much going for myself to let an insecure man bring me down.

I looked down at the time and that's when I noticed that it was ten p.m. I was tired as hell but there was no way I could stay another night in this apartment. After I was done packing my suitcase, I slowly began to head downstairs to wait for my brother to come.

I never thought loving Bryson would end this way, but here I was in the process of leaving the one man that I never thought I could never live without.

I closed my eyes only for me to pop them open again when I heard the front door opening.

My heart skipped a beat, because I knew it was Bryson coming back home.

As Bryson entered into the apartment, he immediately looked down at the suitcase that was stuffed with most of my things.

"Where the fuck are you going?" Bryson asked with anger in his voice.

I squinted my eyes at him before I stood up and told him bitterly that I was leaving him.

Bryson looked as if he had been smacked. I could see the rage in his eyes, which instantly made me take a few steps back. But after he seen the fear on my face he quickly began to calm down as he slowly walked over to where I was standing.

"Please, don't go. I'm sorry for everything that I've done to hurt you. Please forgive me."

As he gently touched my bruised cheek my heart felt as if it was broken into two.

"I love you, what am I going to do without you?" Bryson asked emotionally.

"You will survive, I can't keep allowing you to hurt me, I work all fucking day and night to provide for us and you don't even fucking appreciate it. You rather listen to your dumb ass friends and care about how they see you then what you and I have going on. I don't have the time nor the energy to keep stroking your ego. Yes, I may make more than you, but it's both of our money because we are a fucking team. I can't seem to get your ass to realize that shit. All you do when you come home from work is drink until your sloppy drunk. You won't even clean up the apartment or have me something cooked from working all day and when I try to explain this shit to you, all you want to do is hit me.

"Layla, please I will change, I will do whatever you want me to do. Just don't go." He begged.

There was no going back, our time was now up, and all I wanted to do was move on with my life.

"Bryson I will always love you, but I love myself more," I muttered to him.

Bryson was just about to say something, but the honking of my brother's horn stopped him.

"I have to go," I said softly.

I grabbed my suit case and headed towards the door not even bothering to look back at him.

When I stepped out the door I noticed that it was raining outside. The smell of the rain hit my nose as I tried to run to the car, but Bryson wasn't about to let me leave without a fight. He grabbed me by my arm and yanked me back towards him as he started back telling me how much he was going to change for me, but I had heard that so many times that my heart just wouldn't allow me to believe him.

When Lamar spotted Bryson he immediately got out the car and ran towards us. My eyes grew big as Lamar started going off on Bryson.

"Nigga, I'm going to fuck your ass up for putting your hands on my damn sister."

Bryson didn't even get a chance to get one word out before Lamar punched him square in the jaw which caused Bryson to fall. Next thing you know a fight broke out that neither I nor Promise could break up. Promise and I stood there and watched in horror as Lamar beat Bryson to a pulp.

After Bryson was laid out on the cement, Lamar looked down towards him and once again told him to stay away from me.

"Get your ass in the car, Layla," Lamar demanded.

I already knew what time of day it was. I looked back at Bryson and I sort of felt sorry for him. As he tried standing up from the wet ground, the rain continued to pound down on his beaten body. After sliding into my brother car, he didn't waste any time with speeding out of my apartment complex.

****

THE NEXT DAY

I woke up the next morning to the sun shining in my face. I groaned as I pushed my face down deeper into the pillow. I didn't want to get up, all I wanted to do was lay in bed all day and cry, but there was no way Lamar was going to allow that. A soft knock on my door alerted me that I wasn't up by myself.

"Come in," I said softly.

I placed my bedsheets over my bruised face as I waited to see who was at my door.

Promise came in a few seconds later to tell me that if I was hungry that her and Lamar were downstairs eating breakfast.

"Thank you for letting me know, but I'm just not hungry," I told Promise gently.

Promise was just about to close the door when Lamar big mouth ass yelled out that I better get my ass up and come downstairs. I rolled my eyes and sighed with frustration, but I did what I was told.

After sliding out of bed I headed into the bathroom and that's when I noticed just how hideous I truly looked. My face was even more bruised than last night and I also was now showing bruises on my neck where Bryson had chocked me. There was no way I had enough makeup to cover all these bruises. Instead of trying to hide them I decided to just not give a fuck. I pulled my dreads that were hanging down my back into a ponytail before I hurried to brush my teeth.

After I had taken care of my hygiene I slowly made my way down the stairs to find Lamar and Promise sitting down eating and whispering to one another. I assumed they were talking about me because they quickly became quiet when they saw me coming towards them.

Promise couldn't even look at me, instead, she looked down as she began to play with her grits and eggs.

I headed over to the stove and began to fix me a small plate and was just about to fix me some orange juice when Lamar started to try to make light conversation with me.

"How you feeling this morning sis. Are you going to work today?" Lamar asked curiously.

"I'm doing okay, just sore, but I'm off for the first time in months."

As I took a seat in front of him, he quickly started to shake his head. I knew he was pissed off about how my face was looking.

"I should have killed that nigga," Lamar said cruelly.

"I'm fine Lamar," I managed to choke out.

"No, you're not fine. Did you look at your fucking face and neck this morning? You a damn redbone and you over here looking purple and shit. No man has the right to hit you period. Promise and I have decided that you can live with us for a while until you get yourself another apartment."

"No, I don't want to get in the way with what you and Promise have going on. I'm just going to rent me a hotel for a while until I figure out what I'm going to do."

I could tell by how Lamar was looking at me that he thought I was lying to him.

"There is no way I'm going to have you living in no fucking hotel room when I got a three bedroom. You got your own room and is welcome to stay as long as you like. Sis, don't play with me. I'm not going to let you out of my sight, you aren't about to get back with that nigga, I won't allow it."

I looked over at Promise to see if she even wanted me there. But the look on her face really put my mind at ease.

"I don't know why you over there looking at Promise to see if she approves. She is all for you living here."

"Layla you and I have always gotten along, I don't have a problem with you staying here. Plus, I will have some company around here since your brother always working."

Lamar groaned.

The vibe quickly changed to the point where I felt nothing but hostility coming from them both.

I could tell that a lot of shit was going on between them, but it wasn't my place to try to figure any of it out.

"Promise have you forgotten she a damn RN, she ain't hardly going to be here either, unlike you we have to fucking work."

Promise squinted her eyes at Lamar.

"Nigga, don't come at me like all I do is sit home all fucking day. I have my clothing store that I'm trying to get off the ground. That shit takes time, and I bet you that Layla will be here more than your ass!" Promise yelled.

I quickly cleared my throat to let them know that I was there, but they paid me no mind, instead of sitting there and listening to them throw shots at each other, I decided it was best to dip the fuck out while I could.

I eased from the table and headed back upstairs so I could at least take me a shower. As the hot water pounded down on my sore body I began to wonder if staying here with my brother was even a good idea. I mean clearly, they had some issues going on and I didn't want to be in the middle of none of these little disagreements.

After I had scrubbed my whole body clean I hopped out the shower and dried my body off. I wrapped a big plush towel over my wet body and tiptoed into my bedroom. I dug through my suitcase until I found me a pair of panties and a matching bra. In the distance my cell phone was blasting *Lil' Donald- You Can Do Better*. I already knew it was Bryson calling me.

After sliding on me a pair of grey shorts and a black tank top I decided the best thing to do was to block his ass from calling me. If I didn't block him he was going to continue calling and blowing up my phone. There was nothing for us to talk about and after that ass whooping that my brother had given him I thought that would have kept him far away from me, but I guess I had been wrong.

After I had blocked his number I started to feel somewhat better about my situation. I was finally taking the necessary steps of moving on with my life. I knew in my heart that I was finally doing what was best for me.

The slamming of the front door was what pulled me from my thoughts about me and Bryson. I walked towards my window to look out and that's when I spotted my brother hopping into his car and pulling out of the driveway.

"Promise is everything okay," I asked her as I headed down the stairs.

Promise wiped the tears from her eyes before she nodded to me that everything was fine. My heart instantly broke for her because never had I ever seen her cry before. Whatever that was going on with her and my brother must was something that was emotionally draining her.

"If you want to talk about it, I'm here to listen. Whatever that you tell me, will never be used against you, I said softly to my brother's girlfriends.

She looked up at me and gave me a weak smile.

"I rather not get into it right now. Matter fact I just want to forget it all."

I understood what she was saying so I didn't take any offense to it. As Promise continued to clean up the kitchen I took that time to help her out as well. The struggle of keeping the house running and having hot food on the table was something I was all too familiar with. Just imagine doing all this and working a full-time job it would drive anyone up the wall and have them breaking down into tears and wanting to pull their hair out.

As Promise washed the dishes, I cleaned off the table and threw things into the trash. As we both busied ourselves into the kitchen we got through cleaning up in record time.

"Thank you, Layla, for helping me out, that didn't take long at all."

"When you got someone helping you, it makes a lot of shit easier on you," I stated to her seriously.

She nodded her head in agreement before she headed towards the living room.

"How about we find us a movie on Netflix," Promise said as she cut on the T.V.

"That sounds like a plan. I think that will help us both clear our minds," I told her.

I flopped down on the couch next Promise and leaned back on the couch as Promise flipped through some romance movies on Netflix.

When she finally found a movie that we were both interested in she clicked on it. As the movie began to play that's when Promise leaned her head on my shoulder. The movie was near the end when Promise began to lightly snore. I slid her head off my shoulder and laid her down on the couch. She looked so beautiful and peaceful as she slept. All the hurt and pain that I saw earlier was no longer present. I was just about to head back upstairs when I heard Promise mumbled my name.

I froze because I thought she was awake, but when I turned around she had rolled over on her side and had fell back into a deep sleep. As I headed back towards my bedroom I began to wonder what she was dreaming about that had her calling out my name.

CHAPTER 4

LAMAR

A WEEK LATER...

As I looked down at her perfectly typed resume and as I stared into her pretty brown eyes I knew that I had found the perfect assistant. No more long work hours and no more fighting matches with Promise. I had found the one thing that would put me back in good graces with her.

"You have a very impressive resume Ms. Tasha Louis. I'm honored to have someone as qualified as you on my team."

Ms. Tasha stood up, shook my out stretched hand, and gave me a pretty smile.

"Thank you for giving me this opportunity," she said professionally.

"When can you start?" I asked her inquiringly.

"I can start as soon as possible."

"Perfect, I will need for you to meet me here in my office no later than seven thirty in the morning."

Tasha nodded her head and told me that she would be here.

After she had left out my office I quietly looked back over her resume. The bitch was smart as hell and had a lot of experience with loan accounts just to be twenty years old. The fact that she had worked at American Finance for over a year gave me all the reason to hire her. American Finance was basically the best loan company you could work for. They didn't just hire anyone. I already knew hiring her was the best business decision that I had ever made. But as I placed her resume in my drawer I began to second guess myself.

Tasha wasn't only smart, but the bitch was fine as hell. She wore very little makeup, her hair was long, black, and straight, which she wore down her back. She was dark chocolate in complexion, slim, but was thick in all the right places. I had to stop myself from staring at her throughout the interview, I mean she was just that beautiful with such an innocent face to match. I groaned when I noticed that my manhood was on hard.

"Fuck," I muttered to myself.

I was going to have to get my hormones in check because there was no way I wanted to be getting on hard around her. That was no unprofessional I told myself. Guilt instantly began to set in when I began thinking about Promise and what she would do if she found out that I was getting hard for a fucking twenty-year-old.

I rubbed my hands over my eyes as I tried to take the nasty thoughts from my mind, but I found it hard. I couldn't stop thinking about sucking and licking all over Tasha's young chocolate body. I instantly snapped out of my trance when Kasey appeared at my door. I could tell by how she was looking that she had an attitude and she was pissed off about something.

"So, did you hire little Ms. Chocolate Drop?" she asked with attitude.

"Yes, I hired her. Don't even think about giving her a hard time. Before I let her leave, I will gladly show you to the door. She has way more experience than you do anyway, and I don't get the vibe that she will be keeping up any mess in this office like you have been doing since I first opened my doors."

Kasey's mouth dropped open as she stared at me with anger.

"I don't keep up any mess, if Tia told you this then the bitch lying on me." Kasey defended herself.

I wasn't in the mood to fuss with Kasey. Instead I ignored her comment.

When Kasey noticed I was ignoring her she quickly sprung into action and turned her charm up to level ten.

She walked over to where I was standing I wasn't expecting her to place her hand on my dick print.

"Don't even act like you don't want me because your dick is telling me otherwise. You want me as much as I want you, I don't know why you are still fighting the shit. I can do things that your girl just won't do."

As good as Kasey sounded I knew fucking with her was going to be the end of me. It was something about her that told me to avoid her as much as possible. My mind told me to run, but my dick wanted me to stay and play.

Even though Kasey was fine as hell she was always starting some shit, which was a turn off to myself. One thing I hated the most was a messy ass bitch and Kasey was just that. I was sick and tired of Tia coming to me talking about Kasey and what she was doing to her. The only reason why I didn't get rid of her because I knew she had a family she had to take care of and I didn't have anyone to replace her, now that I had just hired Tasha who was ten times smarter, there was no way I was about to continue to put up with her bullshit.

When Kasey realized that I wasn't playing with her, she quickly snatched her hand away from my crotch, turned on her heels in a huff, and headed back to the front of the office. If she thought I was about to spare her or break her off any of this wood, then she had another thing coming. One wrong move and she was going to be out the door.

LATER THAT DAY...

Before heading home, I decided to do something that I had never done before. I stopped by Kroger's picked up Promise some roses and some of her favorite chocolate candy before making the ten-minute drive home. As I pulled up at my house, I noticed that Layla's black Acura was parked next to Promise's crème Dodge Charger. I was relieved to know that Layla was still at my house and haven't snuck back to her dumb ass boyfriend like she normally did after one night of spending the night with me. Even though my sister was grown I swear she made some stupid decisions at times when it came to love. I'm not going to lie, I've never liked any of her niggas that she used to bring home and introduce to the family. I felt she was too good for all of them but let her tell it they all were the love of her life.

This Bryson nigga was by far the worse of them all. By me being the oldest I wasn't about to let no nigga run over the only sister that I had. After mom and dad died I promised them both on their death beds that I was going to take care of my sister and I was going to keep that promise. If I would have come home to find that she had gone back, I would have hopped back in my car and made a trip to her fucking apartment and dragged her back home with me.

Sometimes people didn't know what was good for them and needed someone to steer them in the right direction when they failed to do it themselves. I was just that brother who was willing to steer Promise in the right direction when I saw she needed my help.

I stepped in the house a few moments later to find Layla laying on the couch sleep while Promise was in the kitchen cooking her famous homemade hamburger and fries.

"Baby I'm home."

Promise turned around and her whole face lit up when she noticed I had a bouquet of roses in my hand along with her favorite Heresy kisses.

I placed a kiss on her beautiful lips, before she embraced me in a hug nearly knocking down her roses out my hand.

"Thank you so much, I love them," Promise said happily.

"Baby, I have some good news for you."

Promise stopped what she was doing and gave me her full attention.

"What's the good news?" Promised asked

"I hired me an assistant today. I'm confident that I will not be having to work all these long hours. The girl I hired just left American Finance, you know its hard to get a job there. She has a lot of experience for her age. She had an amazing resume as well.

"Baby, that's the best news that I've heard all day."

"Tomorrow she will be starting her first day, all I have to do is show her how to use our system and I will be all yours. I'm going to have her working with the older loan accounts while I work with the ones who come in every day."

"Baby, I'm so fucking happy. You just don't know how much I've missed you."

"I can only imagine," I muttered into her ear before placing a kiss on her neck.

I was just about to pull her shorts down so I could dip my tongue in her honey pot, but the sound of Layla moving around in the living room made me pull away.

When Promise eyes met mine I saw nothing but lust in them. She wanted this dick and I was down to break her off some.

"Layla can you do me a favor, can you watch the food while Lamar and have a talk," Promise yelled out to my sister.

"Sure, you know I got you boo!" Layla yelled back.

Promise didn't hesitate to grab me by my hand as we made our way up the stairs to our bedroom.

Just as we made it to our door, Promise placed her hand over her lips to let me know that we had to be quiet.

My sister was a grown ass woman, she knew if she heard some loud moans and yelling that we were probably fucking and to not disturb, but I understood what Promise was trying to do, she didn't want my sister to feel uncomfortable.

As we stepped into the bedroom I made sure to close and lock the door behind myself. I licked my lips as Promise removed her shorts and laid cross our bed. I didn't hesitate to slide between her legs and start placing feather light kisses on her chocolate thighs. Her moans filled my ears as I made love to her with my mouth.

"Baby I want you so fucking bad," Promise moaned sexually.

I pulled away from her and hurried to remove my dick from my black khakis.

I was so ready to bust me a nut that I wasn't even bothered by her giving me any head I was ready to rock her little pussy.

But I already knew Promise wasn't going to allow me to stick until I licked so I went on and gave her some head. I teased her clit with my tongue just before began to suck on her pussy. I slid my tongue in and out of her honey pot as she moaned and cried out my name.

When she started begging me for the wood I didn't even hesitate. I quickly slid into her entrance as she cheered me on.

As I slid in and out of her love box I began to place sweet kisses on her neck as well as her collar bone.

"Fuck me baby," she whispered into my ear.

When I began to go deep she started whimpering, whining, and scratching my back up but that didn't stop me from getting all up in her coochie. She wanted the dick and she was going to get just that. When she started creaming all over my love stick, I grabbed her by her throat and began to slam in and out of her until my dick felt as if it was about to explode. Her nookie was feeling so damn good, but I wasn't ready to bust just yet. I wanted to at least get the chance to hit her ass from the back. Doggy style was by far my favorite position.

When I slid out of her she began to whine that her pussy was getting sore.

"Baby, we been together for two years, you should be use to the dick now," I joked her.

I smacked her on her thigh as I flipped her small ass around.

"Get on your knees baby and arch your back, you already know what time of day it is."

When Promise had gotten into position I first licked her pussy from the back and played with her clit just before I slid my tongue towards her ass crack. I ate her ass as I fingered her pussy. Her loud cries filled the room but there was no way I was finished with her just yet. After I had pleased her with my tongue only then did I slide deep inside her.

"I'm not going to hurt you baby, so relax," I told Promise as I began to slow grind into her.

When Promise had relaxed and her pussy started gripping my dick I decided to play with her titties as I continued to stroke her from the back.

"This dick so fucking good," Promise kept crying out.

"Baby, I'm about to bust," I told Promise as I started to speed up the pace of my strokes. As I went deeper, Promise started crying and screaming.

A few seconds later I filled her kitty kat with my cum.

****

THE NEXT MORNING

I was beginning to think that things with Promise and I was turning around. I woke up to her giving me some morning head. Damn, it wasn't anything better than waking up to your girl sucking your dick. After I had caught my morning nut I kissed her on her cheek and headed to the bathroom, so I could shower and get dressed for work.

After I had taken care of my hygiene I hurried to get dress and headed downstairs, so I could head to work. As I hurried down the stairs I wasn't expecting to smell any breakfast being cook. I nearly fell over when I spotted Layla dressed in her scrubs and Promise still in her bedclothes in the kitchen preparing breakfast together.

"Baby I fixed you a plate. I got it wrapped up for you. Look on the kitchen table." Promise instructed.

I grabbed my plate on the kitchen table and kissed Promise in the mouth and kissed my sister on her cheek.

"Thanks ya'll. I didn't even know I was hungry until I smelled this food cooking in the kitchen."

Promise beamed and poured me a fresh cup of coffee before she shooed me out the door.

"Have a good day baby!" Promise yelled just before I slid inside my car and pulled off.

****

Even though I had just caught me a nut before I had left home that morning, I still found myself eager to bust another one. As I sipped my cup of coffee at my desk I began to try to get my mind off of sex before my new employee came into my office. Ten minutes later I heard a tap at my door.

"Come in."

When my door opened in walked Kasey with Tasha followed right behind her. I could tell the look on Kasey's face that she didn't like Tasha, but I didn't give a rat's ass. All I knew was she better not try no foul shit or she was going to find herself jobless. When Kasey noticed me staring at her with that no-nonsense look she quickly turned away and headed back towards the front of the office leaving Tasha to fend for herself.

"Good Morning, Tasha how are you?" I asked her as she took a seat.

"I'm doing okay, I'm ready to get to work," Tasha said with enthusiasm.

"Well, I'm happy to have you on the team."

I pulled out a folder and grabbed a few papers that needed to be filled out before I could put her behind a loan account.

As she filled out her paperwork, I couldn't stop staring at her. She was dressed in a crème dress that hugged her slim frame and was looking so fucking beautiful. Her dark chocolate complexion seemed to glisten as the sunlight from my window beamed down on her. Her long black hair was pulled back in a ponytail while her sexy full lips were pressed together as she filled out her paperwork.

I began to fidget in my seat because my dick was steady trying to rise. Just staring at her had me aching to stroke my dick. When she stared up at me with her pretty eyes I knew then that I had fucked up by hiring her. This bitch was so fucking fine and by me being weak for a pretty face, I knew I was going to have a hard time being able to work alongside her.

After twenty minutes had gone by that's when Tasha finally passed me her paperwork and told me she was done filling it out. I grabbed the paperwork from her hand and that's when our hands brushed up against each other. Electricity shot up my body and I quickly snatched my hand away from hers. I guess he must have felt the same because she quickly began to fidget in her seat.

After her paperwork was filed I quickly told her to follow me up front so I could show her where she was going to be working at. I secretly thanked the man above that Tasha didn't have to share an office with me. There was no way I was going to be able to sit in the same office with her and be able to get any work done. I refused the hurt Promise no more than I already had.

As I began to show Tasha how to work our software I could feel someone was staring at me. I turned around and sure enough, I noticed Kasey was staring daggers at Tasha and I. I could feel the jealousy pouring out from her. I turned back towards Tasha, so she could get my undivided attention. I had no time to worry about Kasey. Whatever she had going on it was time for her to get over the shit. She only sucked my dick and she was already acting like she had a fucking problem. I only hoped shit didn't get out of hand.

"Do you think you can handle this by yourself?" I asked Tasha with concern.

"Yes, I think I have everything under control."

I looked over at Tia and kindly asked her to help Tasha if she ran into any trouble. I felt that Tia was the only one I could trust to help Tasha out just in case I wasn't available.

This made Kasey roll her eyes at me.

"It's funny how you can ask Tia to help little Mrs. Chocolate drop, but didn't ask me."

"I know just as much as she does," Kasey said crossly.

"Kasey get over yourself, no one cares about your hurt feelings," Tia said with a little attitude.

"Look I don't know what your problem is with me Kasey because I haven't done anything to you. I'm here to do my job and go home every day, so stay in your lane, and there won't be a problem," Tasha said snappily.

I could feel the room heating up and I quickly tried to calm everyone down.

"Kasey come to my office for a minute so I can talk to you," I hissed at her.

"If you need anything here is my extension, I told Tasha as I pointed to a paper that was taped over her computer. You can also ask Tia for help, if for any chance Tia isn't here you can just come knock on my office door and I will answer whatever question you may have."

After Tasha was good and settled in I headed back to my office with Kasey walking behind me.

After we had both made it into my office I closed the door behind myself to make sure Tasha nor Tia heard what was going on.

"What the fuck is your damn problem? I will not allow you to run off my new assistant."

"That bitch don't know what the fuck she is doing. She barely out of high school and you over there practically lusting over her."

"Look I'm not lusting over anyone at this office. I have a beautiful girl at home. I don't want nobody here, I said with confidence."

"Well, apparently your bitch ain't pleasing you if you let me suck your dick. Don't sit here and act like you didn't enjoy what my mouth did to you."

One thing that I couldn't lie about was Kasey's head. Her head was A1 if only she wasn't so ratchet I maybe would have considered coming back for more, but as I stared down at her I knew fucking with her was where I fucked up at.

"Look, that will not be happening ever again. You caught me when I was weak, but you won't catch me slipping again."

Kasey chuckled which caused me to have chills.

She was so close to me that our lips were almost touching.

"If I want more from you, I can have it," Kasey said with confidence.

I pushed her away from me and told her she had to leave.

"Like I said earlier, you will not be sucking my dick again and it was a mistake. Just do me a favor and do your job and don't be trying to do some foul shit. I have no time for this."

This really pissed her off which caused her to go off on me.

"Fuck you Lamar, you want to play games and fuck on that young bitch, then do what you have to do boo, I don't want your little dick ass no way."

I shook my head at her petty ass as she left my office. Kasey wasn't anything but a little thot looking for some side dick that she could control. The only reason why she was pissed was because she wanted me and I didn't show interest that I wanted her back in return. It was an ego thing nothing more to it. The bitch was so angry and in her feelings that she even said my dick was small. We all knew that was a fucking lie.

Eventually, Kasey was going to find her ass another victim that she could manipulate but I wasn't about to be on that list.

CHAPTER 5

PROMISE

(2 WEEKS LATER)

I always heard that a place to a man's heart was being able to cook, being able to fuck him right, and being the type of bitch who could get along with the people he loved. One thing about me, I knew how to cook and I knew how to fuck my man. The only thing that I was lacking was having a friendship with his sister Layla.

Don't get me wrong Layla and I were cool and never had I ever gotten into it with her. She was good people, but we weren't close. It was just a mutual respect that we had for each other. She knew her brother loved me, and I knew that he loved her, so we never once overstepped on our boundaries. Layla was twenty-six and was about two years older than I was. She was very successful to be her age and I admired her determination to succeed. I always had found myself fascinated by how she worked her ass to the bone just to get where she was today.

I know for a fact after Lamar lost his parents less than six months apart due to his mother having kidney cancer and his father had throat cancer, things were hard on them both. I could remember Lamar telling me that his sister was taking it hard after losing their parents and he was worried that she was going to have a mental breakdown, but through it all she got through the tough times and she was on top winning.

I had nothing but admiration and respect for her, so when Lamar told me that he wanted his sister to come live with us until she got back up on her feet, I was all for it. I had no clue that Layla's boyfriend was abusive, but when I saw the bruises on her face and neck I literally felt nothing but sympathy for her. Layla was too fucking beautiful to be suffering the way that she had been. No female deserved that type of treatment and my heart instantly went out to her.

The fact that Layla was always working I rarely ever saw her but during the early mornings. Sometimes, I would hear her coming into the house late at night, but by that time I would be too damn drained to get up to even see how her day had been.

Being in an abusive relationship could be deadly and I could tell from when I would catch a glimpse of Layla that she was suffering inside. She needed a friend and I wanted to be the one who helped her get through her painful situation. I didn't have any friends of my own, I just had never been the type of bitch to keep a whole bunch of bitches in my circle. I kept to myself which kept a lot of drama from my life. I didn't have time for petty bitches and snake ass bitches, but Layla was an exception to the game. If I had to be anyone's friend, it definitely would have been hers.

I made myself a promise to find out the next time that she was off so we could go shopping or even go out for drinks. I never wanted her to feel that she didn't have anyone who would listen to her. Even though Lamar was her brother and he loved her, there was no way she could sit down and have a logical conversation with her brother without him getting into his feelings. Nope Lamar wasn't about to have any of that, it was his way of doing things or no way at all.

So I figured that Layla needed someone she could talk to or at least listen to what she was going through without judging her. I was down to be that person, but that was only if she wanted me to.

Things were beginning to turn around in my life and I was feeling as if everything between Lamar and I were going to be okay. He had finally started coming home at a decent time and he was back dicking me down almost every day. I had no complaints because finally, I had gotten exactly what I had been begging for.

I had been at my clothing store nearly all day and was shocked to see a good little amount of people coming in and buying bags, shoes, jewelry, as well as a large number of clothes. I really was beginning to feel as if my life was finally headed in the right direction. If my clothing store was finally about to hit big that was even more money coming into the house along with what Lamar was bringing home.

After stopping to get some food to cook for that day, I took the ten-minute drive home. I pulled up at my driveway a few moments later only to see that Layla wasn't there. Lamar haven't been lying when he said all Layla did was work. I grabbed the few bags of groceries out my back seat and headed into the house so I could start dinner before Lamar got home at six.

I was on the verge of unpacking when I noticed there was a handwritten note from Layla telling me that she was going to be back home around six that evening that she was called in to do a few hours at the hospital.

That meant that the whole house was going to be full. I didn't have a problem with that I had gotten enough food for everyone. I looked over at the clock and noticed it was nearly three in the afternoon. Well if I wanted to have the food done by the time they got home it was time that I started to prepare my famous pot roast. After I had turned my slow cooker on and had seasoned my pot roast I headed upstairs so I could hop in the shower.

After I had showered and was smelling fresh, I hurried to my closet, so I could find me something sexy to wear. I wanted to attract Lamar's attention tonight and cooking my famous pot roast and wearing something that showed my curves and assets was sure going to lead to a fuck session. My pussy began to tingle just thinking of it.

After over twenty minutes of throwing clothes around in my closet, I finally decided to wear a pair of black lace booty shorts, with a soft pink tank top that didn't leave anything to the imagination. I pulled my weave back into a low ponytail before I sprayed on some perfume and glossed my lips with my favorite lip gloss.

I stared at myself in the mirror and knew that Lamar was going to find me irresistible. As I made my way downstairs that's when I heard my front door open and then close.

"Lamar is that you?" I asked with excitement in my voice.

"No, it's me, Layla."

Layla was dressed in her usual grey scrubs and her freshly twisted dreads pulled back into a low bun. I noticed the bags that she was rocking under her eyes, so I could tell that she hadn't been sleeping.

Layla headed into the living and flopped down on the couch and pulled her black scrubs off her feet before she started making light conversation with me.

"Dammmmnnn, you looking good as hell tonight. Then you got something smelling good ass hell in here," Layla said to me.

"Thank you boo, I just want to look good when Lamar walk through that door. I decided to slow cook a pot roast and veggies tonight for dinner."

"Well, Lamar gonna fall out when he see you tonight." Layla complemented me.

I couldn't help but blush.

"I haven't had food like this since, my parents passed. Bryson he never hardly cooked. Now I see why my brother so crazy about you, you go over and beyond," Layla mumbled.

I gave her a weak smile before I walked over to where she was sitting and took a seat beside her. I could tell that something was bothering her and I was curious to know what it was.

"As long as you living here, I promise that I will have your ass eating good every day."

"I'm going to hold you to that then," Layla said before closing her eyes.

I cleared my throat which got Layla's attention. I always learned growing up if you wanted to know the answer to something then you must first ask the question.

"What's bothering you? Do you want to talk about it?" I asked Layla with concern in my voice.

"Layla, I love Lamar with all my heart and soul, you're his sister, and I don't want you to feel that you have to suffer in silence. I'm here if you ever want to talk or if you just want someone to listen to you. Whatever you tell me I promise I will not say anything to your brother. That's the girl code," I told her gently.

Layla nodded her head at me before we embraced each other in a hug.

"I don't want to bother you with my problems. I will be okay."

"You don't look okay." I told her bluntly.

Layla didn't hesitate to pinch me right above my nipple.

"Ouch," I cried out.

"That shit ain't even hurt, with your little blunt ass." Layla joked

I giggled.

"I'm the realest bitch you will ever know. I'm going to tell you like it is."

"Um I can see that," Layla laughed.

"My brother is so lucky to have you. We should really go out sometimes," Layla suggested.

My eyes twinkled.

"Before you say anything else, I was thinking the same thing," I said honestly.

"Well, I'm down if you down," Layla smiled cheerfully.

For the first time in two weeks I had finally seen Layla smile.

"You work so many hours. So, when could we go out and have a good time?" I asked curiously.

"I can easily take me a weekend off, shid we can party this whole fucking weekend if you want to," Layla suggested.

We laughed and joked around with one another as we tried to decide where we wanted to go this weekend.

"Be ready to have a good time," Layla laughed.

"I'm so ready for this." I joked.

I was just about to head back into the kitchen when my cell phone began to blast *Jazz Cartier.*

I picked up when I saw that it was Lamar calling me.

"Hey baby, If you on your way home, see if you can stop by the liquor store and get a bottle of wine for Layla and me," I said into the phone.

"Baby, I'm calling to tell you that something came up at the office, the new girl that I hired accidently messed up a few loan accounts. I'm here at the office still going back behind her to fix what she messed up. I'm not going to be able to make it home until around nine tonight."

My whole face must have told it all because Layla asked me if I was okay.

Instead of saying anything else to Lamar I decided the best thing to do was end the call. My heart felt as if someone had snatched it right out of my chest. Just when I thought things were going to get better, now I realized that the shit wasn't about to happen anytime soon.

After ending the call, I tightly gripped my phone in my hand as a single tear fell down my cheek. The happy mood that I was just I had been destroyed.

"Promise what in the hell going on? Are you okay?"

I shook my head that I wasn't.

"You may think me and your brother have the perfect relationship, but its far from the truth."

"What are you trying to tell me?" Layla asked with concern on her face.

As I stared into Layla's eyes I couldn't help but see Lamar staring back at me.

I couldn't seem to find the words to speak or even to express myself.

Layla didn't push me for answers, all she did was sit there with me as I cried about her brother.

The smell of the pot roast snapped me out of my trance a few moments later and I headed into the kitchen to find that the roast and veggies were done and ready to eat.

"Layla it's time to eat," I shouted out to her.

After Layla and I fixed our plates, we took a seat at the kitchen table and that's when Layla tried making light conversation with me.

I guess after a while Layla got the hint that I just wasn't in the mood to talk because she finally gave up on the small talk and we both finished our meals in silence.

After dinner was over with that's when Layla grabbed my plate from my shaky hands and told me that she was going to wash the dishes while I went upstairs to relax. I tried arguing with her about it, but she insisted and after a while I decided to listen to her. I headed upstairs, slid into my bed, and flipped on my tv. Twenty minutes later I heard footsteps coming upstairs, at first I thought they were Layla's, but when my bedroom door swung open I was met with Lamar's pretty brown hazel eyes.

"Baby I'm sorry," Lamar started off saying, but instead of listening to him, I quickly muttered that I was going to bed.

Lamar headed into the bathroom and closed the door behind him just as I slid into a deep sleep.

THE NEXT MORNING

I woke up the next morning with stomach pains and the urge to throw up, but I quickly chalked it up to laying down on such a heavy meal the night before. I groaned as I leaned over towards my nightstand and grabbed my phone. I still had twenty minutes before I was due to get up, so I was sort of pissed that I had gotten up before my alarm was set to go off. I slid out of bed and tiptoed downstairs, so I could find me an Alka-Seltzer to settle my stomach. As I mixed my drink I heard some loud banging at my door.

"Layla, I know you in there, open this fucking door!" I heard a man yelling.

I headed into the living room just to see who in the hell was banging at my door at seven in the fucking morning.

That's when I noticed Layla was laying on the couch and rubbing sleep from her eyes.

"Layla please open the door so we can fucking talk. Please don't leave me!" the nigga yelled in a whining high pitch voice.

Layla rose up on the couch and stared at me with fear in her eyes.

That's when the dots connected in my head and I knew then that Bryson was the one yelling at my fucking door like he was crazy.

I could feel the fear radiating from her body, so I took it upon myself to handle the situation.

I opened my door, but I made sure that the screen door was locked firmly.

Bryson was standing there dressed in a pair of grey shorts, a black t-shirt, with a pair of grey and black Air Forces. He paced back and forth on my porch until he realized that he was being watched.

Bryson was average in height and was rocking some dreads that was dyed like a reddish color at his ends. I stared at him for a few moments and that's when I started to understand why Layla had stayed with him for so long. Bryson wasn't ugly not even a little, but the way he did Layla made him the ugliest nigga ever.

"Bryson get the fuck away from my house before I call the law on you!" I told him angrily.

"Look, all I want to do is talk to my girl, tell her to at least unblock me so we can talk about our relationship."

I laughed in his face because this nigga had bumped his head if he thought for one minute that Layla was going to call him or even reach out to him.

"Bryson, I hate to be the one to tell you the bad news, but Layla will not be reaching out to you or coming back to you. What ya'll have is over with, she is moving on to bigger and better things, accept the shit and move on with your life as well."

I didn't hesitate to slam the door in his face.

There was no way I was about to let some shit pop off at my damn house.

Just when I was about to head back into the kitchen that's when I noticed that Layla was on the phone and was actually trying to press charges against Bryson just so he could leave her alone for good.

I didn't stand around to ease drop, instead I headed upstairs. I dug through my closet until I found something that I wanted to wear for that day and hopped in the shower soon after.

After I was done showering, I hurried to get dress, grabbed my bag, and headed downstairs.

"Promise before you go, would you like to go out for drinks tonight. I honestly just want to get out. I'm about to go crazy."

"What about your job? Don't you have to work/"

"Nope, I called them and told them that I wasn't feeling well. So, you and I are officially free to do what we please tonight. I just need to get my mind off things."

I felt everything that she was saying because I was feeling the same way. For once I wanted to go out and just have a good time. I didn't want to think about Lamar and what he wasn't doing. All I wanted to do was forget about my relationship and how fucked up it truly was, was that even a bad thing? I asked myself.

If Layla wanted to go out, then I was down to do just that.

"I'm about to head to the clothing store for a few hours and whenever I get back we can eat and head out to have a little fun."

Layla's eyes began to sparkle, so I knew instantly she was excited.

After telling Layla bye I hopped in my car and sped through town until I pulled up at the mall. The mall wasn't that crowded so it wasn't too hard to find me a parking spot. I waved and said a few hellos as I passed a few customers as I entered inside the Galleria Mall.

After stepping inside the mall, I could smell fresh food being cooked and the many voices of the shoppers. Most of all the well-known stores were located next to one another when you first entered the mall but my store was ducked off from everyone. I hurried to set up for that day and within an hour of opening my doors, that's when my store started to become crowded. I beamed behind the cash register as my clothing store seemed to build beyond capacity. I began to silently thank the man above for finally guiding my mind into thinking of ways to better promote my business.

I had grinded my ass off to get my store to popping and finally it was paying off. I worked over five hours straight with no break and still more people were coming in to purchase anything they could get their hands on.

If my business kept booming like this eventually I was going to be able to expand and even start hiring others to work for me. Just the thought placed a smile on my face. When the clock struck two that's when everyone started to clear out because it was time for me to close the store so I could take me a lunch break. I flipped my open sign to closed before I hopped into my Dodge Charger.

As I cruised through the streets of Warner Robins in search of food I decided to swing by Lamar's job to see if he wanted me to pick him up something to eat while I was out and about.

Ever since he had opened up his own loan company no longer were we able to have lunch together. He started eating through his lunch break instead, but today was going to be different. I was on an all-time high about all the customers that had come in earlier that day and I just wanted to eat lunch with the man so I could talk to him about it.

Ten minutes later I pulled my Dodge Charger next to his all-black Mazda. I took a look at myself in the car mirror before I stepped out my car. I was dressed in a red and white sundress with a pair of red flip flops. I ran my hair through my long weave just before sliding on a pair of my favorite red shades. As soon as I stepped inside Lamar's Loan Company I was met by two of Lamar's employees. Tia smiled at me and we made light conversation with one another, but when my eyes landed on Kasey, I instantly got the vibe that the bitch had an issue with me.

Never did I ever get a good vibe with Kasey since she first started working there, but I always kept my opinion to myself and never addressed my concern to Lamar. Instead I ignored the jealous hoe. I had been around enough bitches in my past to know when a hoe wanted what you had but couldn't have it.

I already knew Tia felt the hostility between Kasey and I because she quickly stepped between it and asked if I was there to see Lamar.

I quickly nodded my head and stepped behind the counter, so I could head towards Lamar's office.

I knocked softly on his door and that's when Lamar glanced up from his desk of paperwork. The young girl who was sitting across from him at his desk turned around from what she was doing and stared up at me.

"Promise, what are you doing here?" Lamar asked curiously as he stood up and walked over to where I was standing.

"I came by to see if we could have lunch together, we ain't did that in forever. I also got good news to tell you. I opened up my store today and I had so many customers that it was barely had enough room for everyone to fit inside.

Lamar's eyes lit up with happiness and I embraced him in a tight hug.

"I really believe that things are about to turn around," I told him with confidence.

He nodded at me before breaking our embrace.

"Baby, I'm so proud of you. I love your motivation to succeed. Keep pushing and your store will be blooming with clients."

After he was done praising me, that's when he finally took a step back and introduced his new assistant Tasha to me.

I stared at her for only a few seconds and knew instantly that something was off. Even though she smiled at me and acted as if she liked me, I knew the bitch was being faker then the weave she had on her head.

I really got in my feelings when the bitch told Lamar that if they didn't hurry to lunch they were going to be late.

I looked at him with my mouth wide open.

"So, I assume you not going to eat lunch with me?" I asked him coldly.

"Baby, it's not that. It's just that Tasha and I already had made lunch plans at AppleBee's we got some paperwork we were going to discuss while we ate," Lamar told me calmly.

I stared from him to Tasha and that's when I noticed the hoe staring at me with a smirk on her face.

I wanted to punch the bitch square in her mouth, but I decided it wasn't even worth it.

I took a few steps back as I stared at him with hate in my eyes.

"I'm glad that you rather put your little assistant before the bitch you live with. Is this the bitch you fucking behind my back?" I asked him loudly.

Lamar looked at me as if I had smacked his ass.

"What the hell are you talking about? Tasha and I are not sleeping together and never will. She is my assistant nothing more."

I was just about to blast his ass, but that's when Kasey walked into Lamar's office.

"I'm sorry to interrupt, but I do hope you know we have customers in the front. If you don't want your business out, try to keep it down," Kasey said to us before turning back around to leave out.

Just when I thought things couldn't get any worse that's when Kasey stopped in her tracks, turned around, and said some shit that almost threw me.

"A lot of shit has been changing since Lamar hired this bitch." Kasey said angrily as she stared at Tasha.

"Who in the hell are you calling a bitch," Tasha asked Kasey angrily.

"I'm talking to your ugly ass hoe. You think you run some shit here because you getting close to Lamar, but you don't run shit bitch." Kasey spat angrily.

Lamar tried to intervene but that's when Kasey began to attack Lamar.

"Nigga you can't tell me shit. All you do is be in your office all day claiming you training this dumb hoe, but you claim you hired her because she was so experienced. Well, I want you to know that I'm not about to work here no longer then I have to. I was going to give you a two weeks' notice, but I don't give two fucks about you or this job. So, I just came in here to tell you that I quit," Kasey said bitterly before turning on her heels and walking out his office.

I felt as if the wind had been knocked out of my chest.

Lamar couldn't even speak that was just how thrown he was from what Kasey had done. The bitch had basically told me in so many words what had been going down since he had hired this little young hoe.

"Well thank you Kasey for letting a bitch know what's up," I said loudly as I stared at Lamar and Tasha.

Tasha tried to speak, but when I looked at her with a deadly look she quickly shut her fucking mouth.

"I'm done with this shit Lamar. I'm sick and tired of the lies."

"Baby, it isn't what you think, whatever you do don't listen to Kasey or any of that crazy shit she just said," Lamar tried telling me, but I wasn't hearing it.

It didn't matter if he was fucking this bitch or not the fact he was spending so much time with her and barely wanted to even have lunch with me was enough to show me who he really cared about and apparently, I wasn't on his list.

I wasn't in the mood to hear any of the shit he was about to say, instead of standing there, I quickly headed out his office, passing Tia on the way.

"Is everything okay?" Tia asked.

As the tears fell from my eyes, I quickly stopped in my tracks and looked at Tia.

"No, nothing is okay and it never will be."

****

I pulled up at my house and headed inside to find Layla in the kitchen cooking. My stomach began to growl as the smell of food hit my nose.

"Layla, you didn't have to do this," I told her sweetly.

"Well, I thought I would do something nice for you. You really helped me out this morning and I appreciate that. Bryson is very determined about what he wants, and you stood up to his ass. That's something that I just couldn't do, I've tried so many times, but I always end up caving and going back to the same bullshit, but not this time. This time things are going to be different."

"No matter what Layla, I'm always going to be in your corner. We have to stick together, these men are about to drive us up the wall with there foolishness.

Layla nodded her head in agreement.

"Why the gloomy face what's bothering you?"

Damn, I thought I had hidden my emotions well, but I guess I was wrong. I tried to lie but I could tell by how Layla was looking at me that it wasn't any point in even doing it.

"I went to Lamar's job today thinking that me and him could maybe eat lunch together, well turns out he had made plans to eat with a new assistant that he had just hired. We sort of got into it because he basically told me that he wasn't going to cancel lunch with his assistant to eat with me. That's when one of his other employees walked in and started throwing hints that he was probably fucking the new girl or at least he wants to."

Layla stared at me with her mouth hung wide open.

I could tell by how she was looking that she was super pissed about what I had just told her.

"Promise don't be stressing over some other bitch, I will talk to him and handle the shit myself."

"Layla you ain't got to do that."

"Well, I'm going to. Now take a seat boo and relax. Let forget about Lamar and all the other bullshit."

I pulled out my kitchen chair and took a seat while she busied herself with fixing me a plate. Layla was so right and I appreciated that she had calmed me all the way down.

I licked my lips when I spotted she had cooked spaghetti and meatballs with french beans and a slice of garlic bread toast.

"Damn, this smells so good," I told her as I took a big bite of my food.

I closed my eyes as my mouth basked in the favor of the spaghetti.

"This is so delicious what in the hell did you put in this food?"

Layla took a bite and laughed.

"It's my secret recipe."

I put down my fork and stared at her with squinted eyes.

"Um, aren't you going to share it with me?"

"If I do, I will have to kill you," she joked.

I rolled my eyes at her comment before kicking her under the table.

We both burst out laughing just before we started back chowing down on our food.

I was half done with my plate when I stood up and asked her if she wanted anything to drink.

She quickly nodded her head at me and that's when I headed towards the fridge and pulled out a bottle of red wine and poured us both a full glass.

I wanted to at least get a chance to drink a full glass of wine before I became too full. After Layla and I had finished our meal we sipped on our wine. We laughed and talked to one another until Layla invited me up to her bedroom.

Victoria secrets had lingerie on sale last week so I brought two. I wanted to try them on and I wanted your honest opinion of how I look in them.

I told her that I was willing to give her my honest opinion because I never sugar coated anything. She wanted honesty she had the right friend.

I grabbed my glass of wine and followed her up the stairs to her bedroom. I took a seat on her bed as she pulled out her Victoria Secret's bad from her dresser drawer.

"Before you try on your new lingerie I got a question."

Layla faced me and gave me her undivided attention.

"I'm curious to know who are you going to be wearing this shit for?" I asked her bluntly in a joking manner.

"Just because I don't have a man, don't mean I can't still continue to buy myself lingerie. Who knows I may meet someone, this shit will come in handy then."

I laughed at her ass so hard that I began to tear up.

"Will you stop damn joking me and let me try on this shit in peace/" Layla asked with a smirk on her face.

"Okay, no more jokes."

"I hope you don't mind me undressing in front of you."

"We both females, so nall I don't have a problem."

Layla nodded her head before she turned her back towards me and started to remove first her shirt and her shorts. She next unsnapped her bra and pulled down her panties. I sat there on the bed and stared at her completely naked body. I couldn't tear my eyes away from her even when I tried. Never had I ever been sexually attracted to any female but Layla was different. Her honey-smooth complexion looked smooth as butter. My pussy began to tingle as I thought about her and me kissing and caressing each other bodies.

I was such in a trance that I didn't even hear her calling out my name.

"Promise did you hear me? Can you snap up this bra for me in the back."

I stood up slowly from the bed as I walked over to where she was standing at her. Her long dreads covered nearly her whole back so I lifted them up and pushed them to the side so I could fasten her bra.

"Thank you," she said before she finally turned around for me to see how she looked with her new under on. She was dressed in a hot red bra with a hot red thong that fitted her ass perfectly. She looked like a damn sexy red apple that was ready to be devoured.

"So do you like it?" Layla asked me.

Her soft hazel brown eyes penetrated my soul as she waited for my answer.

"I love it on you, it really compliments your complexion and your eye color," I told her as I tried to pull my eyes away from her.

Layla must have noticed the intense staring that I was doing because that's when she walked over to where I was standing and kissed me on my lips.

I nearly passed out right then and there.

"Thanks for telling me the truth," Layla said before grabbing her clothes that she had just taken off and heading into her bathroom.

I touched my lips and stared back at the bathroom door that Layla had just closed behind her. I still couldn't wrap my mind around what had just occurred.

Layla had just kissed me and my ass liked it.

CHAPTER 6

LAMAR

2 Days later...

My life was really starting to get out of control. I always had the feeling that Kasey would one day make a scene and act crazy as hell, but never did I ever think the bitch would do it this soon. This bitch had ran her fucking mouth like a water faucet and had walked slam off her job. My home life was in fucking shambles because of what she had damn said. Promise was up here thinking I was fucking on my damn assistant Tasha when I haven't even touched the girl.

Now, I'm not going to lie, I had been watching her sexy ass strutting around the office and I had noticed how she would flirt with me and shit, but never did I play into any of the shit. I felt as if I had my temptation under control for the most part. Tasha was only twenty she was a baby in my eyes. She wasn't anywhere near ready for a man like myself, at least that was what I thought, but how she had been looking and dressing since I had hired her I could be so fucking wrong.

I groaned as I placed my face into my hands. I had barely slept for the past two nights because Promise had my ass sleeping on the fucking couch. When Layla pulled me to the side this morning and told me that Promise was very upset about some shit that she had found out about me, I quickly sat my baby sister down and explained everything to her. I trusted my sister with my life because never had she once ever betrayed me. I had no one I could talk to about what was truly going on in my head but her. After I told her most of what was going on she gave me some A1 advice that I just wasn't ready to take.

I groaned in frustration because I felt as if I had no control over my life. My thoughts were running wild, but it immediately came to a halt when my phone began to vibrate in my pocket. I pulled my phone out not expecting to see Layla name on my screen. I picked up without hesitating just to see what was going on with her.

"Bro, you really need to get your shit together. You really breaking Promise's heart."

My heart began to feel heavy because never did I ever want to hurt Promise but the desire to be deep in another bitch's pussy was really beginning to fuck with me. I loved my ass some Promise, but sometimes I found myself craving a little something extra on the side. Never did I want to cheat on Promise, but I always found myself in positions that led to it.

"Layla I've tried talking to Promise, she won't talk to me, she keeps avoiding me, so how can I fix some shit if she don't even want to hear a nigga out."

Layla became quiet until I heard her car door open then close.

"I took off work yesterday because she was depressed, and I was worried about her. I have to take my ass to work today and I'm working double shifts. Whatever you got going on with that bitch at that office cut that shit short and come home to check on Promise. Don't fuck this shit up bro, you got you a good girl. Leave the other bitch alone, they can't give you what Promise gives you. That girl loves you, so do right by her, she deserves that shit."

I listened to every word that came out of my baby sister's mouth, but as soon as our called ended that's when Tasha took that time to walk her ass up in my office dressed in a beige skin-tight dress that didn't leave anything to the imagination.

Her perfume filled my nose as she walked her fine ass towards me.

"Lamar I just wanted to drop off these folders for you to file. I finally completed and closed each of the loan accounts that you gave me."

"Thank you, Tasha, for helping me out, you really have given me a lighter workload."

"Of course boss man, that's the job of the assistant. Is there anything else I can help you with before I head to lunch?"

I nearly dropped the folders from out my hand when she spoke that statement. The way she looked at me and had the nerve to bite down on her bottom lip spoke volumes to me. I tried looking away, but I just couldn't her beauty was just that fucking mind-blowing.

When she began to rub her soft hands up and down my arm, I quickly became tense because she was way to fucking close and I didn't want to do some shit that I would later regret.

I cleared my throat and told her that I had to make a quick phone call, but she quickly grabbed the phone out my hand and placed it back in the cradle before she began to massage my neck and shoulders.

"You are so tense, you need to relax, and let me take good care of you," Tasha whispered into my ear before she began to massage out the kinks.

I closed my eyes and decided to relax. She was only giving me a massage it wasn't like she was trying to fuck me. A few moments later that's when her hand fell from my shoulders and neck. My eyes popped open when I felt her hands between my legs.

I tried pushing her hand away, but Tasha wasn't bothered by that, she was persistent that she was going to get this dick.

"What about Tia?" I asked her just before she began to unbuckle my belt.

"She just left for her lunch break, it's just you and me," Tasha spoke with a thick sexy voice.

I groaned as she slid my now hard dick out my boxers and began to rub it up and down with her hands before she began to slide me in and out of her hungry mouth.

I moaned lowly, as she worked her tongue around my mushroom head just before she began to suck on my love stick like a lollipop. Tasha's mouth was on point and she knew exactly what she was doing. This little bitch had experience and I was curious to know if the pussy was just as good. Even though I had promised myself to never fuck anyone on the job or give them the dick I was about to break all the rules for Tasha. My dick needed attention and I was going to give it just that.

There was no way I was about to miss out on getting my dick wet from this beauty, so I quickly pushed her head farther down on my pole until I heard her gag. A few seconds later I pulled her head up for air just before I stood up and pushed her up against my desk. I pulled her tight dress above her hips and pulled her black thong to the side. I played her pussy with my fingers until she was dripping wet and begging for the dick.

I caressed my manhood around her entrance for a few moments, before I finally slid between her folds. She gasped loudly as her tight little pussy began to clench around my thickness. I didn't move the first few moments, I wanted her to get adjusted to my thickness and I didn't want to rush because I knew I wouldn't be able to hold my nut in.

I began to slow stroke her from the back as I gradually made my way to her chest and started playing with her plump titties. Her soft moans had a nigga wanting to fuck her harder, but I knew that shit wasn't possible. Babygirl could barely take this dick, but I wasn't going to let that stop me from catching my nut. As I went deeper, she tried running, but it wasn't even about to go down. She had been low key flirting and now that she was finally getting what she wanted she was trying to run from it. Nah, no running bitch, I thought to myself.

"Fuck," Tasha cried out as I began to slow grind into her love tunnel.

When she began squirting and nutting on my dick I slid out of her and turned her around so she could face me. I placed a kiss on her cheek before sitting her back on the desk. I slid between her thighs as I began to fill her up with my hard dick. I sucked on each of her hard nipples as I stroked her to a steady pace.

Sweat dripped from my brow as I tried to penetrate her very soul. Her loud cries filled my ears which brought me closer to nutting. A few moments later, I slid into her one last time before spilling my seed into her tight sugary walls.

There were no words spoken to her about her keeping her mouth shut. Tasha was far from dumb and was smarter than the average twenty-year-old. After we had both cleaned ourselves up and had put back on our clothes that's when I heard Tia stepping back into the office.

"You should get back, don't want Tia thinking something," I muttered in her ear.

She nodded her head just before she slid her tongue into my mouth. We kissed until we both came up for air. She grabbed a few folders off my desk that I haven't gotten around to logging in and told me that she was going to log them into the system for me.

After she had left out my office I couldn't help but sit there with a smile on my face. Damn, that bitch pussy had drained every little bit of energy that I had in my body.

As I stared down at my paperwork I could barely concentrate. That pussy had a nigga all in his head and I couldn't stop thinking about her. Tasha was only the second bitch that I had blessed with this dick, the first girl I had actually given the dick to was my ex Amber, Kasey big mouth ass didn't count because I didn't bless her with the dick. There was no way I was going to fuck Kasey anyway, she couldn't keep her mouth closed and keep shit just strictly business.

I got a different vibe with Tasha, she gave off the impression that she could pull any man that she wanted. She was very confident, didn't need a nigga to do shit for her, and was just looking for a little dick. She wasn't trying to be with a nigga or fuck up my happy home with Promise.

"Would I fuck Tasha again?" I asked myself.

I would be lying if I said that I wouldn't. If the opportunity presented itself. I was going to continue to dick Tasha down as long as she kept her mouth shut and kept our secret to herself.

The day seemed to fly by and before I knew it, the clock struck five and Tia came into my office to let me know she was getting ready to leave. I thanked her for working her ass off like I did every evening and told her to get home safely. She nodded her head at me and told me she would see me in the morning. Ten minutes later that's when Tasha finally came to my door and knocked on it gently.

"Mr. Lamar, I just finished the other accounts you gave me earlier. I just wanted to tell you that I'm heading out," she spoke professionally.

A nigga had to stop what I was doing just so I could get a good look at the girl who had me almost pussy whipped. My dick began to jump as soon as she stepped all the way into the room.

"Do you need me to do anything for you before I leave?" Tasha asked seductively.

I tried to nod my head at her, but my body wouldn't cooperate. Tasha smirked at me as she took my silence as the okay to get down on her knees. I wanted to push her away from me because there was no way my dick could take fucking her twice in one day. Her pussy had a nigga having withdrawals for her. Normally I could control myself better than this, but it was something about Tasha that had fucked me all the way up.

She didn't hesitate to pull my dick out and began making love to it with her mouth.

I rubbed my hands into her long weave as she began to deep throat me. The sounds she was making was only making my dick harder by the second. I groaned when she pulled my wet dick out her mouth and started sucking on each of my balls. Her tongue wasn't a joke and she knew how to use that bitch. I flicked my thumb around one of her nipples before tightly teasing it as she continued to suck and please me.

Before she slid my dick into her mouth again she spit on it and began to rub it up and down with her hands. I closed my eyes and nearly came when she sucked my dick into her mouth like a vacuum.

"Fuck, yes, suck this dick girl," I urged her.

My eyes popped open a few moments later and I stared into her eyes until I felt as if I was about to explode.

"I'm about to cum," I choked out.

I pushed Tasha hands off my dick and pulled my rod out her mouth just before I painted her beautiful face.

After my dick was drained of my cum, that's only when Tasha got off her knees and headed towards the bathroom to clean her face off. After she was all cleaned up, I already knew that it was time for me to take my ass home. There was no way I was going to be able to stay at work and concentrate, plus I didn't want to go home late and find Promise pissed with me yet again.

"I'm about to head home Mr. Lamar I hope you enjoy the rest of your night," Tasha said before placing a kiss on my cheek.

That was what had me fascinated over her young ass. This bitch could fuck me, have me cumming in loads, and then act as calm and cool like nothing had just happened. If I didn't still have the side effects of busting in her face I would have thought none of this had even happened today.

I locked my office and locked the building up with Tasha following right behind me. I waited until she had hopped into her silver Benz and had pulled away before I stepped into my car and headed home. As I made the fifteen-minute ride home, I couldn't shake Tasha out of mind, her charisma was what had pulled me in from the jump. I knew nothing about her, only that she had been a bookkeeper at American Finance before she applied as my assistant.

To be honest I didn't even know where she lived or who she lived with. All I knew was she was pushing an updated Benz and always came to work looking drop dead gorgeous. As I pulled up at my crib, I came up to the assumption that whoever Benz she was pushing weren't her own. I didn't pay her that fucking much to be able to afford a damn 2018 Benz. Either the bitch had a sugar daddy or was living home with her pops and maybe it was his car.

Just trying to figure Tasha out was making my head hurt. I pushed her to the back of my mind because there was no way I wanted to have another bitch on my brain when I was around Promise. She knew me to fucking well to even come at her half stepping.

After I stepped out my car I headed inside my crib to find my sister and Promise, preparing dinner while vibing to Travis Scott. I stood and watched them for the longest time without them even knowing it. Just knowing my sister and my girl was getting along relieved a lot of stress. Promise got along well with anyone, but I knew at times Layla personality could be a little too much to deal with. Having a bitch that could get along with my sister was a keeper. For the first time in a long time I began to really look at Promise and notice just how perfect she truly was. She was everything that I wanted in a woman and still I was out getting my dick wet by other bitches.

"I'm home," I spoke loudly so they could hear me over Travis Scott.

Promise turned around first and I could see the shock in her eyes when she noticed that I was home before it was dark.

I could still feel the coldness from her, but I didn't give a fuck, I walked over to her and tried to embrace her in a hug but she quickly pushed me away from her.

"Don't even fucking think that you are about to come up in here smelling like sex and rocking damn lipstick on your shirt.

"I felt as if Promise had slapped a nigga in my face.

"Baby, I ain't been fucking," I lied.

Promise laughed at me just before she began to attack me. Next thing I knew shit started flying at me and there stood Layla looking in the distance as the shit went down.

"Nigga, you smell just like the fucking bitch. And you got fucking lipstick on your fucking shirt!" Promise screamed.

I looked down at my shirt and sure enough there was a small amount of Tasha's lipstick that must had smeared on me while we were fucking earlier that day.

I noticed the tears falling from Promise's cheek and I instantly felt nothing but guilt. I had fucked up this time and I had no clue if I could even make shit right with her.

Layla didn't say shit to my defense, but I knew she wasn't going to. She had already told me what the deal was and I haven't even listened to her ass.

Promise dropped the plate that she had in her hand and I watched it as it shattered on the kitchen floor. The smell of our dinner burning was enough to snap Layla into motion and to cut the stove off.

"Baby," I tried speaking.

But I quickly shut my mouth when I noticed how Promise was looking at me. I swear I felt as if that bitch could murder me with her eyes.

"Did you fuck that bitch? Promise asked me.

I kept denying her accusation, but I soon told her the truth when she told me that she was going to kill my ass if I didn't stop lying to her. After I came clean that's when Promise wiped the last bit of tears from her eyes and stared me dead in the eye.

"This that you and I had is over with," Promise spoke calmly.

No longer was she screaming which had a nigga feeling like she was going to murk my ass for real if I made one wrong move.

"As soon as I find me somewhere to go I will be leaving you," Promise spoked coldly.

As Promise stepped over the broken dishes and the broken kitchen chairs, I tried stopping her, but she quickly snatched away from me. She looked at me and I instantly stepped back from her ass.

"Nigga don't fucking touch me, don't ever touch me again," Promise spat furiously before making her way up the long flight of stairs.

I stared at Layla and she just shook her head at me, with the I told you expression.

"Sis, I fucked up bad," I cried to her.

"Yeah, you sure fucking did and the sad thing is, there is nothing I can do or say to make this shit turn in your favor," Layla told me.

I wanted to beg Layla to help me try to win Promise back, but I knew there was nothing that my baby sister could do. My relationship had been hanging on by my promise to never hurt her ever again, now that the promise was broken the relationship that I took for granted no longer existed.

I headed towards the kitchen and poured me a glass of Jack Daniels. I needed something to calm my nerves down because I wasn't expecting shit to go down like it had. I still couldn't get over how Promise looked when she told me she was going to find her an apartment and leave my ass. It took time to sometimes to find an apartment so I felt as if I had time to do whatever I could to win Promise back.

I took a seat on the couch and turned on the TV but nothing interested me enough to take my mind off the girl who I loved with all my heart.

My plan was to keep shit professional between Tasha and I. What we had done today could never happen again, I told myself. If I wanted my girl back I had to do what I had to do to win her back to me. I wasn't going to give up.

I stared at the TV close to two hours before I notice that Promise and Layla had gotten dressed and was heading out the door.

Promise was dressed in a skin-tight red dress that she had only worn with me once. The dress was short and stopped a little below her thigh.

If she bent over I already knew she would give some nigga a good view. Her back was completely out as well and I could tell that she wasn't wearing a bra either. Her red stilettos completed her outfit and had my imagination running wild. Her lips were painted pink and her makeup was perfect on her beautiful chocolate skin. Her bone straighten weave fell pass her ass and she looked like she could be a Barbie doll. That dress left nothing to the imagination and I instantly began to get sick to my stomach just thinking about what Promise was about to do.

Layla had the same type of dress but hers was black and she was rocking a lime green pair of stilettos with hers. My sister had her dreads curly which flowed down her back and her makeup was flawless as well.

"Where are ya'll going?" I asked them both.

Promise rolled her eyes at me, so I knew she wasn't going to tell my ass shit. It was Layla who spoke up and told me that they were going out for drinks and to not wait up for either one of them.

I nearly fell over because there was no way I wanted either one of them to step out the fucking house looking like they were, but I already knew neither one was going to listen to me. Promise was pissed about me betraying her and my sister had to leave the one man whom she thought she was going to spend the rest of her life with because he wasn't man enough to deal with her success.

Both women were dealing with the pain and hurt of something that a nigga had done to them. There was nothing that I could say to either one of them to change their mind.

The only thing that came out of my mouth was for them to be safe. As the door closed I poured me another glass of Jack Daniels and sipped on my drink as I began to wonder what Promise was really going to do tonight.

Nothing, my mind told me. Promise loves you, she just angry and upset, she isn't going to go cheat on you, Your baby sister is there she will make sure that Promise don't take this shit to far, I reasoned with myself, but as I continued to drink and as it became later, my confidence of the love Promise and I use to have begun to evaporate.

I sipped and cried almost the whole night and not once did I hear the front door open. I called Promise and Layla back to back, but neither one picked up the phone. When the clock struck one in the morning, I knew that neither one wasn't going to come home anytime soon. Instead of waiting up for them to come through the door, sleep finally found me and I passed out on the living room couch.

CHAPTER 7

LAYLA

I don't know what had come over me or what I was thinking when I kissed Promise on her lips. She was my fucking girl, but I just couldn't resist the urge to kiss her. Never had I ever wanted a female, but it was something about Promise that had me ready to explore my sexuality with her. Just when I thought she was going to push me away or better yet curse my ass out she shocked me when she didn't even mention it or bring it up to me.

She left the shit alone and I did the same. Me kissing her was something that we didn't bring up or discuss. But still deep down inside I still felt the chemistry that her and I shared.

Silence filled the car as I cruised the dark streets of Warner Robins. It was time that Promise and I got out for a while and had us some fun. I pulled up across the street from my favorite bar, parked my car, and hopped out. Every time I came to the bar I always had to park across the street because their parking lot would be packed to the max.

Promise and I waited until the traffic had subsided before we ran cross the road toward the bar that I normally went to when I wasn't working. The bar was deep as fuck but luckily, we found us a seat and waited for the bartender to take our order. *21 Savage* played in the background as the niggas shot pool in the nearby distance. After we downed our gin and tonics that's when we signaled to the bartender to keep them coming.

The goal for tonight was to get fucked up and forget about all the shit that we were going through. My heart went out to Promise as I watched her sip on her drink. She was deeply in love with my brother, but he was too fucking dumb to understand that he had a good thing.

Well I take that back, my brother was far from dumb, but he basically felt that Promise wasn't going to leave him no matter what he did and that was where he was so wrong. I was a bitch, so I knew how women thought, I tried to tell him that he was fucking up, but as usual his heard headed ass didn't listen to me.

Even though Promise was barely able to keep it together, niggas were still eyeing her up. When I spotted a nigga walking towards us, I lightly tapped Promise on the thigh to let her know that we had company. She placed her glass down as we waited for this nigga to approach us. The bar was rather dark, so we couldn't really make out his features until he was standing in front of us.

"How are you beautiful ladies doing? My name is Ken. What are ya'll names," he asked us sweetly.

Me being the type of bitch that I was, I gave this nigga two fake names and watched as his eyes grazed over Promise's body.

Ken was dressed in a pair of blue jeans skinny legs, a black shirt, with a pair of black Jordans on his feet. He flashed us a smile and I saw nothing but gold in his mouth. I wasn't the type of bitch who found thug ass niggas attractive and I guess Promise wasn't interested because she kindly told the nigga that she was married. I wanted to spit out my drink because the nigga was thirsty to get to know Promise. She wasn't giving this nigga any play and he finally got the hint and walked off secretly seething with anger from getting turned around.

After he was out of earshot Promise and I started laughing hard as hell.

"Damn, we hell," Promise slurred.

"Promise how in the hell you drunk already? You only had four drinks and you already slurring."

Promise gave me a sad face.

"I forgot to mention that I can't hold my liquor that's part of the reason why I never go out and drink."

I rolled my eyes at her comment and took her glass from her.

"Layla, what the fuck are you doing? I was drinking that."

"Um, I know I said we were going to get fucked up, but I'm not trying to carry your ass to the car. You have reached your damn limit. You look like you gonna fall out any minute."

Promise huffed and folded her arms over her chest.

"I'm not fucked up yet, I want to leave this bitch barely able to feel my face" Promise laughed before snatching her glass out of my hand.

I eyed her ass up as she drowned the last of her drink and told the bartender to pour her another one.

I shook my head at her and turnt my glass up as well.

Promise was right, the goal for tonight was to get fucked up and forget about the niggas who had done us dirty.

"All I want to do is forget about your cheating ass brother," Promise said emotionally.

I continued to sip on my gin and tonic as she began to give me the run down with her and my brother. I nearly fell out my chair when she started talking about he cheated on her with his ex- girlfriend Amber the one who killed his baby back in college.

I swear when I saw Lamar I was going to beat the fuck out of him, I didn't know what in the hell he had going on to want to fuck with that white hoe again. No way would I want to stick any bitch who killed my seed. Apparently, my brother was lost because he was making some fucked up decisions.

I saw the hurt in her eyes as Promise started telling me just how much she loved my brother and how he just didn't love her enough to be faithful.

"Promise listen, I know my brother has done a lot of fucked up shit to you, but he doesn't know what the hell he's doing, he's lost and he's still trying to find himself."

"But he hurting me in the process Layla, I can't keep going through this shit, and you can't tell me that I should."

I placed my finger gently on her chin to lift her head up so I could stare into her eyes.

"What type of bitch do you take me for? I would never tell you to stay with my brother if you didn't want to. Yes, Lamar is my brother and I love him to death but wrong is wrong."

When the tears began to fall that's when I took it upon myself to console her. I embraced her in a hug and rubbed my hands through her hair as her whole body began to shake.

When *Lil' Donald-Do Better* began to play in the distance. She pulled away from me, wiped her eyes, and began to rap to the song.

You fell in love with a fuck nigga, now you feel like you can't trust niggas

You the one that went and stuck wit em, I know you knew he was a fuck nigga

Why you let em do you like that, why you let em do you like that

You leave once and be right back, why you let em do you like that

You let em cheat on ya, you let em beat on ya

You scared to be single huh, you need to leave homie

He call you ugly names, yo mind ain't feeling the same

You're going through bodily change, girl get back on yo game

Friends try to tell you leave him, but you feeling like you need him

He can cheat right in yo face and you still gon believe him

Then a good man come along, and you push em away (push him away)

You push em away (you push him away) you gotta do better

I nodded my head to the music and watched Promise as she began to move her body in the seat.

After Lil' Donald song went off that's when I noticed Promise whole attitude had changed. No longer was she crying about Lamar, instead, when I tried to mention her issue with him, she told me she was over the bullshit, and she was going to leave the shit alone.

I was just about to say more but she cut me off when she switched the subject.

"OMG, I love this bar Layla, we have to come here again, "Promise said into my ear.

I nodded my head at her as my drink began to kick in, a bitch was fucked up and didn't even know it.

When the bartender made the announcement that they were going to close in twenty minutes I knew it was time to wrap all this shit up.

Promise was already torn up, but she insisted that we were going to take at least three more shots before we dipped out for the night. There was no way that either one of us was going to be able to drive back home. It was a ten-minute drive from the bar to the house and I wasn't even going to trust myself to get behind the wheel.

The best thing that came to my drunk filled mind was to call a damn taxi to come to scoop our drunk asses up and take us home.

After we had taken our three shots to the head, I gently nudged Promise to let her know that it was time for us to go.

We held on to each other as we headed out of the bar. After we made it to the car which was parked across the road from the bar, we slid inside, and slammed the door behind us.

"Layla I'm so fucked up."

I looked over at Promise and laughed at her ass.

"I'm not far behind your ass. There is no way that I can get us home, so I think the best thing to do is try to call a taxi."

Just when I was about to pull out my phone that's when Promise snatched it out of my hand.

"Before you call a taxi, I just want to tell you thank you for taking me out tonight. You could have gone to work or did some other shit, but here you are."

"Promise you and I are more alike than you can imagine. Our hearts are both broken by the men whom we thought would love us unconditionally. No matter what happens, you will never be alone. I'm your friend and I'm always going to be here whenever you need me."

"I've never had a friend that I could ever trust," Promise said sadly.

"Babygirl, I don't know who you use to fuck with, but I swear to you I'm different. You will never have to worry about me trying to hurt you. If you ever need to talk or if you want to go out to clear your mind, you already know that I'm down to come along with you."

I was just about to call the Taxi when I noticed that I had over five missed calls all from Lamar.

"Why are you looking like that?" Promised asked curiously.

"Oh, It's just Lamar, he called me five times," I told her.

Promised rolled her eyes.

"He called me ten times, I wasn't bothered, and I didn't pick up either phone call or text message."

I exited out of my missed calls and got in touch with a taxi who told me that he would be there in less than fifteen minutes to pick us up.

As we waited on the taxi I turned on the radio and that's when *H-Town* began to blast from my speakers.

Promise closed her eyes and began to hum to *Knockin' Da Boots*.

I stared over at her and couldn't stop thinking about just how beautiful she truly was. I had never been with another woman or ever had a desire to be with a girl. As I stared at Promise's full lips I wanted to know just how they would feel on my body. When I glanced down at her titties which looked as if they were about to fall out her dress, I began to question myself at that very moment.

It had been over four weeks since I had last had any type of sex. Me and Bryson's relationship had gotten just that bad that we weren't even fucking before I left his ass and moved in with my brother. I needed some type of release, so I blamed the desire that I was feeling inside on my hormones or it could have been the liquor, there was no way that I was really feeling these feelings about my brother's girl.

I was so in my head about the shit that I didn't even know that Promise had caught me watching her. She leaned towards me, pushed one of my dreads that had slipped from my ponytail out of my face, and placed a soft kiss on my cheek.

"I've been wanting to do this since you first kissed me the other day," Promise whispered into my ear.

I couldn't move, I mean I felt as if I was frozen because this had to be a fucking dream. But as Promise and I stared into each other eyes I knew that this wasn't a dream at her. When our lips connected I felt as if my whole body was on fire. I sucked on her bottom lip as I began to lightly caress her body with my free hand.

My tongue ring danced in her mouth as I took that time to be bold enough to pull her titties out of her dress and began to flick my finger around her nipples.

Silk-Meeting In My Bedroom began to play in the distance as Promise and I kissed and caressed each other bodies.

I pulled away from her first and Promise pulled my ass back towards her.

"My pussy is on fucking fire, and I want you to put the shit out," Promise slurred into my ear.

I was drunk, but I wasn't as wasted as Promise was. I could have pushed Promise off of me and told her that I couldn't give her what she wanted, but I didn't do any of this shit because I wanted to taste her and give her exactly what she had asked for.

"Are you sure you want this?" I asked her gently.

"Yes, I want this Layla," Promise said passionately.

That was all I needed to hear before I began to lick and suck on each of her nipples until she was calling out of my name. After I was done showing her nipples some attention, I kissed and sucked on her neck as I played with her pussy. Her kitty kat was dripping wet and I was eager to slide between her thighs and make her cum.

I opened my side of the door and walked over to the passenger side where she was sitting at. She opened the door for me and lifted her dress up so I could get to work. I was just about to dip my tongue inside for a taste when I noticed the cab coming down the road. I stood up from my position and hurried to pull Promise's dress down before the taxi pulled up next to my car.

"Fuck," Promise wined as she looked up towards me.

Just when I thought shit was about to go down that's when the taxi pulls up. Promise slid out of the car and I made sure to lock it just before we slid into the back seat of the taxi. After I had given the driver the directions to where we wanted to be dropped off, Promise started rubbing her soft hands up and down my thighs.

I snapped my head up and noticed that the taxi driver wasn't bothered by what we were doing in the backseat. He had his earplugs in his ear and was having a conversation on his phone. I looked towards Promise and saw nothing but lust in her eyes.

"Relax, let me please you," she whispered into my ear before flicking her tongue around my earlobe.

I closed my eyes and moaned softly as she pushed my thighs apart and pushed my thong to the side. As our lips connected Promise dipped her finger into my honey box. My juice box was dripping wet and I was eager for a release.

When she slid two more fingers into my love box, I was near the brink of cumming. Her hot tongue caressed my neck and then my ear lobe as she continued to finger fuck me.

I closed my eyes tightly and grabbed the armrest as I softly moaned out Promise's name.

"Your pussy is soaking wet," Promise whispered into my ear before she pulled her fingers out of me.

I grew, even more, wetter as I watched her lick my juices off her fingers.

"Shhhh," she told me gently before she dipped her fingers back into my love box.

As I grinded my pussy on her fingers, she took that time to suck on each of my nipples.

Still, the taxi driver had no clue what in the hell we were doing in his backseat. It was pitch-dark which left us hidden from his view.

I never thought that a female could ever make me cum, but I had been so terribly wrong.

As my body started to shake and as the cum dripped from out my coochie Promise slid her tongue deep into my mouth.

A few moments later after I had pulled down my dress that's was when we pulled up at our destination. Promise pulled out her wallet and gave the driver some cash all while he was on the phone begging his girl to get back with him.

I shook my head at his ass and hurried out of the car. Hearing any man begging his girl to get back with him was something I didn't want to hear because I knew he had probably done some fucked up shit to her to make her want to leave in the first place.

I looked towards the house and noticed it was pitch dark inside, that only meant one thing, Lamar had finally gone to sleep. I looked down at my phone and noticed it was two in the morning. I followed Promise inside the house and that's where we spotted Lamar passed out on the couch with two bottles of booze next to him.

Promise and I stared at one another before she placed her hands over her lips. I nodded my head letting her know that I understood what she was saying. We both tiptoed up the stairs towards my room and that's where I embraced Promise in a hug.

Even though we had left the bar fucked up I was beginning to come off some of the high that I was once feeling.

"Damn tonight has been wild, but I've enjoyed every minute of it," Promise said softly.

After pushing her gently up against the wall my mouth found her pretty soft lips. As we kissed, I gently gripped her by her hair and deepened our connection.

We pulled back from one another a few moments later and that's when we told each other goodnight. I watched her as she headed out of my room and headed towards her own. I closed the door behind her, fell straight into my bed, and passed out a few minutes later.

CHAPTER 8

PROMISE

The next morning...

I woke up the next morning to the sun shining in my face with a bad headache. I laid there in utter disbelief as everything from the bar and the ride home in the taxi began to replay in my head. What I had done was wrong on so many levels, I couldn't believe that I had fingered my man's sister in the back seat of a fucking taxi. Apparently, I had drunk way too many drinks because I had fucked around and had done some shit that I never would have thought of doing if I had been sober.

Never have I ever desired another female, but it was something about Layla that turned me all the way on. She had such an amazing personality and had come into my life when I felt as I if I had no one I could talk to. Even though Lamar was her brother not once had she taken sides or gotten involved. She listened to me and my problems without judging and that was all I ever wanted. Even though I looked at Layla as a close friend I would have been dumb to not see just how sexy she truly was. Her features were similar to Lamar's and the fact that she was a redbone and rocked dreads was something else that I found very attractive.

I still felt bad that I had overstepped my damn boundaries and had let the alcohol overtake my body. I was embarrassed, and I had no clue of knowing how in the hell she was going to act when we saw one another again. Even though we had both acted normal the first time she kissed me, this time was so much different. We had gone way too fucking far.

What really bothered me was what would happen if Lamar found out about last night. Just thinking about Lamar put me in a bad mood.

"Fuck him," I muttered to myself as I rubbed the last bit of sleep from my eyes.

I slid out of the bed that I now shared alone and headed to the bathroom, so I could shower.

Since I had found out that Lamar had cheated on me with his assistant I had kicked his ass out of our room. He was now sleeping on the couch which was where he was going to stay for a very long time. I didn't want the nigga touching me or being anywhere near me. I was tired of taking this nigga back only for him to hurt me yet again. I shouldn't have taken him back after he cheated on me with that white bitch, I told myself as I began to wash my body down with my favorite Dove soap.

After my body was good and clean I hopped out the shower and wrapped a towel around myself. I brushed my teeth, pulled my weave into a high bun, and headed into my bedroom so I could put on me some clothes for that day.

I searched throughout my closet until I decided to put on a pair of khaki booty shorts with no panties and a black tank top with no bra. I slid on me a pair of all black socks just before I slid my feet into my Nike Sandals. I rubbed a little CarMax on my lips before heading downstairs to find that the house was empty.

I was secretly happy that no one was home with me because there was no way I wanted to face Lamar knowing I had finger fucked his sister and I didn't want to face Layla knowing that I had initiated the whole thing.

I was just about to open the fridge when my phone buzzed in my pocket.

My heart began to pound because I had no clue who could be texting me at nine in the morning. When I saw Layla's name on the screen my heart skipped a beat and my palms began to sweat. I took a few deep breaths before I finally got the courage to open the text up.

I hope you feeling okay this morning. We need to talk about a few things when I get home. I was called into work this morning, it was last minute., It's a circus up here. I will be home as soon as I can.

After reading the text message nearly five times I quickly slid the phone in my pocket and debated if I wanted to open the store for that day. I needed to find something to do so I could take my mind off Layla. If I sat home I was only going to drive myself crazy wondering what she wanted to talk to me about.

After pouring me a glass of orange juice and draining my cup empty, I decided that I was going to open my shop. My store normally opened three days out the week and it always opened around ten or eleven in the morning. There was no point in staying home. I was going to go make me some money instead. After I had dressed in my favorite pair of ripped blue jeans, along with a pink top, and my pink and white New Balances, I grabbed my purse and headed out the door.

I just about pulled on my driveway when my phone began to ring. I grabbed my phone out my purse and ignored the call when I noticed it was Lamar calling me. There wasn't shit that him and I had to discuss. The whole ride to my store my phone kept going off and I ignore it each time. If he wanted to hoe around on me then I was going to let him, we were done. It was nothing that him and I could do to work this shit out. He had fucked me over for the last time.

I pulled up at my store ten minutes later and hopped out. After I stepped inside I began to set up for that day and just like last time my store was filled up to capacity. I felt the only reason why a lot of people didn't come to my store because they didn't know it existed, it was ducked off from mostly where everything was at. I smiled as I thank Facebook in my head for locating me some potential customers. Facebook ads really had given me a come up.

I had just finished ringing out my first customer when a young ass dude came up to me and asked me if I sold any lingerie. I stared at him because he didn't appear to me like the type to be wanting to be caught in a female store. He was tall, slim, dark in complexion, he was a dread head, and was covered with a shit load of tattoos. He was sexy as hell and had a baby face to match.

I led him over to the other side of the store which was almost like another Victoria secrets and pointed him to the area that he was looking for.

He politely told me thank you.

"If you need any help just let me know."

I was about to leave when he asked me to help pick out something that he could get for his girlfriend.

I was all about being professional and helping customers so when he told me to stay I agreed.

"Do you know what size she wears?" I asked him curiously.

"Um, she wears a medium."

I pointed him towards the side that had nothing but mediums and that was when he picked up a few.

"Which one would you wear?" the dude asked me.

I could tell this nigga was attracted to me by how he was looking at me, but instead of me entertaining it I decided to ignore it. I picked a few of the colors that I liked, and he quickly brought all five of them without giving it a second thought.

"Will this be it for you are do you want to look around the store a little bit more?"

"Nah, I think this will be it."

"Your girlfriend will love these. She is lucky to have someone like you to come and pick her out something sexy to wear."

The young dude beamed before he started making light conversation with me.

"My girl just started working as an accounting assistant at Lamar's Loan Company. She has been working a lot lately, so I decided to do something nice for her tonight, to make her feel special."

I almost fell over nearly knocking down the big box of hangers that was sitting on the counter, next to the cash register.

"Be careful," the dude said as he stared at me.

I placed a fake smile on my face, but I was literally burning up inside. The bitch he was talking about was the same bitch who was fucking my man. I wanted to tell this nigga so badly the real reason that bitch was working so late, but I decided to leave the shit alone. If he didn't know his bitch was cheating, then maybe he wasn't doing what he was supposed to do anyway. If you paid attention to your significant other red flags would be going off in your head when shit wasn't adding up with them.

After the dude had left, my whole vibe had changed. Even though I was deep in my feelings about Lamar and that bitch Tasha, I decided to stay my ass at work so I could get my paper for that day. There was no way I was about to let Lamar win. No way was I going to let him have that much control over me.

I worked my ass off until five that evening and that was when I finally decided to close my shop down for that day. After leaving my store I headed to Kroger's so I could pick up some dinner to cook for that night. As much as I loved working for myself and owning my own clothing store my next love was cooking. Even though I was pissed at Lamar and didn't want to have shit to do with him I was still going to continue to cook regardless. I wasn't about to let no nigga steal my joy. After I had gotten everything I needed from Kroger's I head home so I could put dinner on. I pulled up in my driveway twenty minutes later not expecting to see Layla home so early.

My heartbeat began to speed up as I started to wonder what was going to happen next. Layla was home and we were alone. Lamar was nowhere to be found as usual. I only prayed that shit didn't get out of hand. I sat in the car a little while longer as I gave myself a pep talk. After I was confident enough to head inside the house only then did I step out the car. I grabbed my bags from the back seat and was just about to pull out my house key when the door swung open.

There stood Layla looking sexier than ever. I could tell by how she was sweating that she had been exercising. Her dreads were pulled back from her beautiful face and she was dressed in a pair of black yoga pants with a pink sports bra to match.

"I didn't know you were going to be home so early," I said as I squeezed past her and headed inside.

"I'm shocked as well, I thought I was going to be working until eleven tonight," Layla told me as she started to help me unpack the groceries.

When our hands touched I felt as if the breath had been knocked from my body. I tried giving Layla a weak smile, but it didn't go as planned. The tension was so thick I felt as if I could cut it with a knife.

Here we were in the kitchen by ourselves, but neither one of us was ready to bring up about what was happening between us. Instead, we began to make small talk with one another.

"So, what are you cooking for tonight?" Layla asked as she took a seat at the kitchen table.

"I was thinking about cooking tacos," I told her as I cut on the stove and began to start prepping the food.

"Sounds good to me," Layla told me.

I could feel Layla's eyes on me, but I was doing everything in my power to ignore it.

After over fifteen minutes of silence, it was finally broken when Layla told me that we needed to talk. I stopped what I was doing and slowly turned around to face her.

"About last night and the other day, I just wanted to say" …

But I quickly cut her off.

"Layla stop right there. I was the one who initiated the shit so I'm the one who should be saying that I'm sorry for overstepping the boundaries. I've never been attracted to a female, I'm not…"

I couldn't even get the words out of my mouth which must have caught Layla by surprise.

She stood up and walked over to where I was standing and began to lightly caress my cheek.

"Promise I feel the same way, but something happened between us the other day and then last night. Neither one of us can explain what we are feeling, but I will tell you this, what happened between us in the back seat of that taxi will be our secret. I will never say anything to my brother. It will break his heart if he ever found out."

My whole body felt as if a weight had been lifted off my shoulder. The stress of Lamar finding out was something that I didn't any longer have to worry about.

Just when I thought the conversation was over with, that's when Layla told me that she had some more shit that she had to get off her chest.

Instead of continuing to cook the ground beef, I decided to turn off the stove just so I could give Layla my undivided attention.

"I can't stop thinking about you, I've never felt this way about a female before, it's just something about you that makes me feel safe," Layla admitted.

As she began to trace my lips with her finger that's when my inner freak decided to come out. I opened my mouth and slid her finger inside as I gently began to suck on it.

Her reaction was priceless. I saw nothing but desire in her eyes and I knew what Layla and I felt was a mutual infatuation for one another. Our actions and feelings had nothing to do with our alcohol consumption because we were both sober.

I could tell by how she was looking at me that she wanted me just as much as I wanted her. After she slid her finger out my mouth she quickly replaced it with her tongue. Her tongue ring dance with my tongue as she began to stroke the rest of my body with her soft hands. There was no stopping us now and there was no going back either. Even though I knew it was wrong, I didn't give two fucks about stopping what was happening.

When we came up for air that's when we finally decided to head upstairs so we could really have some fun with one another.

As soon as we made it into my room, that's when we started kissing on one another and that's when the clothes started dropping to the floor. After we were both naked, Layla instructed me to lay across the bed. I did as I was told and didn't dare question her. I bit down on my lower lip as I waited for her to dip her long tongue into my honey pot. I whimpered when she started placing feather light kisses over my entire body. After she had kissed my body up and down that's when she started licking on each of my nipples while she gently stroked my love box.

"Shittt," I moaned out as she began to suck on each of my nipples as if she was a newborn baby. My body was heated, and I was ready for her to make me cum.

As she sucked on my neck, my pussy started to drip. When she slid my thighs apart, I already knew it was about to go down. I cried loudly when she flicked her tongue over my clit just before she slid a finger into my love box. I pinched on both of my nipples as Layla sucked and teased my clit. After she had given my clit the attention that it deserved that's when she removed her finger out my love box and replaced it with her tongue.

"Fuck!" I yelled out.

I pushed her head deeper into my pussy and almost came at that very moment. She ate and sucked on my honey box as if was her last meal. When she pulled away from me, I took that time to dig into my nightstand and pull out my dildo that I had purchased for myself a few months prior. I only had used this vibrator only once but today it was about to finally put in some work.

I was just about to turn the vibrator on but that's when Layla took it from me and turned it on herself. I gasped when she placed the vibrator near my clit just as she dipped her tongue back into my wet overflowing river.

I cried out her name repeatedly as she made love to me with her tongue. Just when I felt as if I was about to cum that's when she removed the vibrator and slid it into my love box. I gripped the sheets to the bed as she slid the vibrator in and out of my tight little coochie.

"I'm about to cum," I cried out as I grinded my pussy on the toy that she was using.

"That's it babygirl, give me all that nut," she said to me as I reached my peak.

When I squirted all over the dildo, Layla smiled down at me.

She stared into my lust filled eyes just before she licked my dildo clean.

I watched her and was so turned by just how nasty she could be.

My pussy began to quiver just thinking about what her mouth had just done to me.

"Come here baby, I'm not done with you yet," Layla said sexually.

I crawled over to where she was now laying on the bed and that's when her and I got into a position where we both could be pleased. When she told me to ride her face, you already know that I was down to do whatever.

After we both had gotten in the sixty-nine position that's when I started to show her just what my tongue could really do. I licked and slurped on her juices as she squeezed and licked the crack of my ass.

I dipped my tongue inside her pie and licked her until I tasted her sweet nectar in my mouth. After we both had reached our peak we kissed each other gently on the lips before we both slid off the bed.

"I'm heading to the room to shower, you can come if you want," Layla said before winking at me.

I blushed as I watched her leave out of my room.

I hurried to put back on my clothes and made sure to spray my room down with some air freshener just to kill the smell of sex. After everything seemed to be in place I headed back downstairs so I could finish cooking dinner for that night.

CHAPTER 9

LAYLA

When my brother first offered for me to live with him I had no intentions of betraying him and sleeping with his girl. I was just trying to lay my head somewhere until I figured out what I was going to do about Bryson. If someone would have told me that I was going to fall in love with a female and she was going to be my brother's girl, I would have laughed in their face, but here I was lying in bed with the only girl that I wanted to be with. Promise and I were both broken by the men who we thought loved us. People always said that things always happened for a reason. The love that we were so desperately was trying to give to our boyfriends we were now giving it to each other.

It was a Saturday morning, my brother was at work as usual, and there was no one here but me and Promise. As we laid next to one another we began to talk about a future together. At first, we were joking, but then the conversation deepened into something that I never expected.

"I want to leave him. There is no way I can be with him knowing that I've fallen in love with you." Promise admitted.

Love was such a powerful word but when she said the three letter words to me, I swear I felt it in my soul because deep down I already knew that I was falling in love with her as well. I wanted for us to be together, but I also knew that I was living in a fairytale.

"I have something to say, but I don't want you to freak out, or anything."

"Spit it out, I want to know what you got on your mind," I told her truthfully.

"I've been thinking that since I'm not going to work things out with Lamar and you since still haven't found you a place yet, we could roommate and get us an apartment together. I honestly don't want to move out and be by myself just yet," Promise said softly.

I kissed her gently on her cheek before telling her that I was down with moving in with her if that was what she wanted to do.

Promise's eyes began to twinkle as she started talking to me about some apartments that she thought I would like. After almost a two-hour conversation about apartments, Promise talked me into getting dressed and heading out so we could go site seeing some of the locations. I agreed because finding us somewhere to rent was important. I no longer wanted to be in my brother's house while sucking his girl's pussy in the bedroom that they used to share with one another.

After we were both dressed, we hopped into my black Acura and headed to look at some of the complexes that Promise thought would be nice to live. We visited close to five apartment complexes before I found the one I wanted to move to. As soon as we drove up in the complex I felt the vibe that this was going to be our new home. Promise grabbed me by my hand as I kept my left hand on the wheel.

"Baby, this apartment complex is amazing. The complex had two swimming pools, a volleyball court, a golf course, a basketball court, a laundry mat and a car wash. The landscaping was on point and it was a gated community as well."

"I wonder if someone is working today that we can talk to about these apartments," I asked Promise.

"Shid, someone may be here, we should go see."

After we had driven around the little community we headed back up front and followed the signs to lead us to the office. As we pulled up in front of the office sign we were shocked to see a few cars already parked out front.

Promise and I looked towards each other and hopped out the car and headed inside. The leasing office was clean and smelled of lemons when we stepped inside. We were met by a smiling lady who introduced herself as Sally. She was eager to let us know that she had a few two-bedroom apartments as well as one bedroom's that was available to move in at that very moment.

"Which apartment will you ladies be interested in?" Sally asked as she slid her glasses on top of her nose.

Promise and I looked at one another and nodded our heads before telling her we wanted a one bedroom.

Sally nodded her head before she handed us an application to fill out.

"All I need is for you both to fill this application out, bring proof of income, and eighty-five dollars, so it can pay for ya'll background checks. You can move in when I have all this information."

She shook our hands and told us that she would hopefully see us soon.

We started filling the application out as soon as we got home.

"The sooner we hurry to get this application turned in the quicker I can get the fuck away from Lamar." Promise said.

I nodded my head in agreement.

After the application was filled out Promise snatched my keys from off the kitchen table and told me that we were going out.

"Where in the hell are we going its almost eight p.m.?" I asked Promise curiously.

"I'm taking you on an adventure," Promise joked before she pushed me out the door.

I was just about to hop in the car when Promise stopped me in my tracks.

"Close your eye beautiful," she told me tenderly.

"Why Promise? What are you trying to do?"

"Will your ass stop questioning me and just do what I say."

I huffed and mumbled under my breath but closed my eyes like I was told.

When I felt a cloth covering my face that's when I heard Promise's voice in my ear.

"Relax babygirl, I'm about to take you somewhere that will take your breath away."

Just hearing her ass saying some shit like that to me, sent chills up my spine. I slid into my car with her help and waited until Promise took me to our destination.

The whole ride to our destination Promise was trying to give me hints on where she was taking me, but I had yet to guess the right answer.

When the car came to a stop about thirty minutes later I began to wonder where in the hell we were at. I was relieved when she pulled the black cloth from over my eyes, so I could see.

I wasn't expecting to be staring at the prettiest lake that I had ever seen. The sun was beginning to set and it looked so beautiful. Promise grabbed me by the hand as we walked towards the deck and took a seat. She laid her head on my shoulder as we both watched the sun go down.

****

A FEW HOURS LATER

After leaving the lake Promise and I didn't head straight home. Even though Lamar was blowing up both of our phones we both decided to ignore his calls. Instead of going home like we should have we decided to go out and have a few drinks instead. We pulled up at a bar not far from the house and headed inside. This bar wasn't as packed as the last one we had gone to. We ordered us a cocktail with rum. As we sipped on our drinks we danced in our seats as the music blasted from the speakers.

As *Shy Glizzy-White Girl* blasted from the speaker me and Promise started singing along.

In love with a white girl

She's soft as powder

I get hard around her

I whip her right here

She French, I'm a coke boy

Don't fuck with broke boys

She know I'm a dope boy

She said give me dough, boy

In love with a white girl

She's soft as powder

I get hard around her

I whip her right here

She French, I'm a coke boy

Don't fuck with broke boys

She know I'm a dope boy

She said give me dough, boy.

I was so into the song that I had no clue that someone was watching me. I nearly fell out my chair when I spotted Bryson staring at me. My heart began to pound as he walked over to where I was sitting.

"Layla I'm not coming to cause any problems I just wanted to talk to you for a minute."

I looked over at Promise and knew instantly she didn't want me talking to him, but I decided that it was time for us to get the closure that we both deserved.

"Follow me outside, you have five minutes to say what you have to say," I told him over the loud music.

"Promise I will be right back, I need to handle this shit."

Promise nodded her head at me and began to sip the rest of her drink as she watched me and Bryson's head out the front door. As soon as my face hit the hot muggy air that's when Bryson started spilling everything that was on his mind.

"Layla, I just want to first say that I'm sorry for everything I've done to hurt you. I admit I've been super selfish and I know I can't take any of this shit back, but all I'm asking you to do is forgive me. I just want to take the time to explain myself finally. When you got on your feet and your career started popping I just felt you didn't need a nigga help anymore. You were self-sufficient, you could do everything yourself, and I just felt left in the wind. You were just taking off and I felt as if I was losing you."

"You never lost me, Bryson, I was right there with you the whole time. You were just to blind to see the love that I was showing you."

Bryson nodded his head at me before he started caressing his finger over my cheek.

"If we never get back together, I want you to know that you will always be my first love. I'm sorry I couldn't show you the same love in return that you gave me."

A single tear fell from my eyes and he quickly wiped it away.

He placed a small kiss on my cheek before moving away from me.

I watched in utter shock as he hopped into his car and pulled off.

I stood there for the longest moment as I tried to get my emotions in check before I headed back into the bar.

When I sat back down with Promise I already knew she was going to want to know what happened and after I had ordered my last drink for that night I gladly told her how things had gone down.

"Baby, I'm glad that you got everything handled, now you can really move on with your life."

"Yes, you right. I can move on, but I can't have the person that I truly want."

Promise squinted her eyes at me and that's when I told her the truth. The shit that her and I were doing wasn't right, but I didn't give a fuck about who it was going to hurt. I wanted what I wanted but I also was a realistic bitch, I knew that our little perfect fantasy was going to come to end.

"What the hell are you talking about?" Promised asked with a little too much aggression.

"Promise its time that we start being honest with ourselves. Even though Bryson and I are no longer together and he has let me go that doesn't mean that we can automatically live this happily ever after fairytale. Promise you already know that even if you do leave my brother we still aren't going to be able to be together. He will literally hurt us both. I'm not saying we can't move in together and be roommates, I'm down if you are, but I know it can never be an us in a relationship."

I could see the tears forming in Promise's eyes, but I wasn't prepared for her outburst.

"How the fuck can you sit here and say some shit like that to me after we have fucked almost every chance we have gotten? How can you say we can never be together when we both know life wouldn't be hitting on shit if we went our separate ways? What he doesn't know won't hurt him," Promise said sternly.

"You aren't thinking realistically. My brother isn't slow, he will eventually put two and two together and then what's going to happen? I will lose the last bit of family that I have left."

Promise stood up and pulled out her money to pay for our drinks.

"Where are you going?" I asked her as she began to walk toward the front door.

"Oh, I don't want you to lose the last bit of your family," Promise said angrily before she left me sitting at the bar to think about what I had just said.

THE NEXT MORNING

The blasting of my alarm clock woke me from a deep sleep. It was time for me to get my ass up and head to the hospital to work a 12-hour shift. I had no clue on how I was going to get through today knowing that Promise and I were at odds with one another. Since we had started fucking around never had we ever gotten upset with one another until last night. Promise wanted us to be together and I wanted the same, but I knew what we had was never going to sit well with Lamar.

I slid out of bed and headed towards the bathroom, so I could get ready for work that day. After I had hopped out the shower and had brushed my teeth, I headed back into my bedroom, so I could find me a pair of scrubs that I could put on for that day. As I began to get myself dressed, that's when I finally noticed nothing but sadness in my eyes.

I had practically come home and had cried myself to sleep last night. Just knowing you were in love with someone that you could never be with them really was fucking me up inside. Instead of harping on my hurt feelings I decided to push my pain aside so I could get my mind right for work. Whatever Promise and I had going on was going to have to wait until I got back home from doing my job, I told myself.

After I was satisfied with my appearance I hurried out my room, down the stairs, and out the door. Lamar had already left for that morning, but as usual Promise was the only one who was probably still in bed sleeping like a baby. I hurried to my car and hopped inside as I peeled out the driveway. If I didn't speed the process up, I was going to be late to work. There was no way in hell I wanted any write-ups.

I already had two in my folder, one was for me being late, and the second one was for not coming in and not calling in time to let anyone know that I wasn't coming.

Never was I ever late for work or had ever missed a day at work, but after leaving Bryson I felt as if my life was falling apart. I had no clue that Promise was going to come into my life and flipped my world upside down either. My mother always used to tell me to always expect the unexpected, falling in love with my brother's girl was very unexpected indeed.

I pulled up at my job twenty minutes later and headed inside. Already the hospital was busy as hell, so I didn't waste any time clocking in and getting my ass to work. It seemed as if time was moving slower than usual and I was irritated more than ever. All I wanted to do was go home and get in my bed, but I couldn't do that today. Today, it was for me to save as many lives that I could and I couldn't let my heart come between that.

I was doing my daily rounds when I heard my name being called over the income.

Layla Martin, please report to the front, the Indian lady who I couldn't pronounce name spoke into the intercom.

Instead of going to check on my last patient I gave my clipboard to my assistant nurse and told her to check on the patient to make sure if they needed anything. My nurse assistant shook her head and headed towards the patient's room while I headed towards the front. My heart almost fell out my chest when I spotted Promise standing there posted up at the front desk waiting for me. She was dressed in a pair of baby blue shorts, a white top, with a pair of white flip flops. Her hair was pulled back from her face in a high ponytail and her face was fresh of makeup. I could smell her sweet perfume as soon as I walked over to her.

"What are you doing here?" I asked Promise with a shocked expression on my face.

"Layla we seriously need to talk," Promise whispered to me.

I already knew exactly what she meant because I felt the same way. We needed to talk, and we needed to talk right then, there was no way I was going to make it through the day without knowing what was going to happen between Promise and I.

"Follow me, we can go outside. I don't want none of these nosy ass bitches to be in my business," I told Promise in a low voice.

When we made it outside, Promise followed me to my car and that's when the conversation started.

'I first just want to say that I'm sorry about last night. I was being very selfish not really thinking about how this will affect you, me, and Lamar."

Promise was just about to say more, but I cut her off.

"Promise, you have nothing to be sorry for. I shouldn't have said the shit so coldly to you. I want you just as much as you want me, but at the same time we both have to think about Lamar and what he will do if he learns that we have both betrayed him."

I noticed a few tears falling from her eyes, but I wiped them away.

"Baby, don't cry. We will think of something. The first thing we need to be doing is move in together. We just need to tread lightly with Lamar, I don't want to do nothing to set him off." I told Promise gently.

Promise nodded her head and that's when she finally looked into my eyes.

"I never thought that I could feel this way about another female".

"I never thought I could either," I admitted to Promise.

"So are we good?" Promise asked me.

"Of course we are. We always going to be good no matter what happens between us. I will be home around seven thirty tonight, maybe we can eat and catch a Netflix movie on TV."

"That sounds good to me," Promise said with excitement in her voice.

"Well let me let you get back to saving lives," Promise joked before she started to walk away.

Hold up aren't you forgetting something? I asked her.

Promise's eyes began to sparkle when she walked back over to me and placed a soft kiss on my lips, I love you baby, she told me before walking back towards her car and pulling off.

CHAPTER 10

LAMAR

A week later...

I had just stepped inside my loan company, when I was met with loud screaming. I stood there in utter shock as I noticed Tasha hands covering her mouth with a nigga on bended knee with a ring box in his hands. Tia looked on in disbelief as she watched to see what was going to happen next.

"Baby, I know we have both hurt each other these past three years that we have been together, but I just want to tell you that I forgive you and I want to spend the rest of my life with you. I want to show you just how much I love you. Will you marry me?" The mystery man asked.

Tears fell down Tasha's eyes as she nodded her head and told him that she would. That's when he slid the ring on her shaky finger and embraced her in a tight hug. They were so engrossed in their lovefest that no one noticed me standing there.

Tia was the one who finally tore her eyes away from the happy couple who was showering each other with kisses and asked me if I saw what had just happened. I nodded my head at her to let her know that I had seen every bit of it.

I felt as if I had been kicked in my stomach because Tasha had never told me anything about her dating someone else. But I had been so pressed on sex that I haven't even thought to ask her. To be honest, it really didn't matter, but I was hurt because I knew that fucking her now was out of the question. One thing that I didn't want to do was get myself involved with Tasha knowing that she was about to get married. I didn't want that heat on me. Tasha must have seen the hurt in my eyes because she quickly kissed her nigga on the cheek before walking over towards me.

"Congrats on your engagement," I told her.

"Thanks," Tasha replied.

"Look, I know I never told you about him but.."

"Don't even worry about it. As long as you happy that's all that matter."

Tasha nodded her head as she stared up at me.

"Well, I'm about to head into the office and get some work done. I hope this won't interfere with your work for today."

"Of course not, I will be getting to work in a few minutes," Tasha muttered before turning around and heading back over to her lover.

I should have known a bitch that fine already had a nigga at home, I sort of had that feeling she wasn't single when I noticed she was pushing a damn Benz when I knew she wasn't making that type of money to afford that type of car. Well, everything happened for a reason, it was probably for the best that I left Tasha alone anyway.

After I had stepped into my own personal domain, I quickly closed the door behind me, and took a seat behind my desk. I felt like shit. I had lost the bitch I loved with all my heart. Tears fell from my eyes as

I sat down at my desk at work. My life felt worthless knowing that I wouldn't have Promise love anymore.

Even though we were still living in the same house Promise always made sure she avoided me at all costs. The fact that she didn't put me out had me thinking we were going to work things out but I had been wrong about that shit.

This morning when I woke up, my heartfelt crushed when I spotted an apartment application. Apparently, Promise wasn't lying when she told me that she was leaving my ass. I was even more hurt when I flipped through the application and spotted my sister information listed on the application as well.

The fact that Promise had gotten super close to my sister was what cut me like a knife. Here I was thinking blood was thicker than water but apparently, I had been wrong.

Seeing that they both were planning on leaving me just didn't sit right with me. I felt betrayed by my damn sister, but I knew Promise leaving me had everything to do with me and my unfaithfulness. I guess the universe was finally giving me what I deserved. I had fucked over Promise for the last time.

A gentle knock at the door pulled me out of my thoughts about my love life. When I looked up I wasn't expecting to see Tasha standing with a pile of paperwork in her hand. To be honest, I surely thought she was going to dip the fuck out without me knowing so she could spend the rest of her engagement with her lover, but I had been wrong.

She was here working, just like she had told me that she was going to do.

"Um, I just wanted to drop some things off to you. We had a crowd up front, I guess a lot of people trying to borrow some money because school is rolling around next month."

I grabbed the paperwork from Tasha's hand as I nodded my head in agreement. I couldn't help but glance at the big rock that was on her skinny finger. Damn, that nigga must have had that bread to afford a ring like that I thought to myself.

Before I could get too deep in my thoughts that's when Tasha interrupted them.

"Are you going to be okay?" Tasha asked gently before she walked over to where I was sitting.

If it haven't been for Tasha, there was no way that I would have gotten through the past week. With my life in shambles, I could barely concentrate let alone actually keep all the accounts in check.

"I'm going to be alright," I muttered.

Tasha cleared her throat to get my attention, but I couldn't even look at her. Just looking at her only brought back all the reasons why I cheated on Promise in the first place.

I know this isn't my business or anything and I had my doubts about telling you, but I think you have the right to know about your girl.

"What are you talking about?" I asked Tasha in confusion.

Tasha bit down on her lower lip before spilling the tea.

"Last week, on my lunch break, I took a friend to the ER to drop her off. I spotted your girl there and she wasn't alone. She was in the parking lot talking to some female. The female worked there apparently because she was wearing scrubs like she was a doctor or either a nurse."

I nodded my head as I waited for Tasha to get to the point.

"I saw her and the girl kissing," Tasha muttered.

"Huh?" I said with confusion.

I had to make sure that I was hearing Tasha correctly because there was no way that my girl was kissing on some other bitch.

"I saw her kissing on some female in the parking lot Lamar, I have no reason to lie to you."

"Look Tasha are you sure that you saw my girl, because one thing I do know, my girl isn't gay and never have been, so you must have gotten her confused with someone else."

Tasha shook her head and pulled out her iPhone.

"I figured you were going to think that I was lying to you, but I will show you myself."

I waited until Tasha found what she was looking for on her phone. When she handed it to me my heart wasn't ready for what I was about to see. I stared at the picture for the longest moment hoping what I was seeing wasn't real, but there was no point in lying to myself. Tasha had been right, in that picture was Promise and my sister Layla kissing one another.

A nigga was hurt and I didn't want to believe the girl that I loved with all my heart could be kissing on my damn sister. I handed Tasha back her phone and stared into the distance. She was talking to me, but I couldn't make out anything that she was saying. I was still in shock about what I had seen. When she finally left out my office and headed back towards her work station, only then did I break down and cry.

When twelve thirty hit, I knew there was no way that I was able to stay to work. I had to get the fuck out of there before I lost my mind. After I had wiped the tears from my eyes, I stood up and headed out of my office.

"Where are you going?" Tasha and Tia asked in union.

"I'm taking the rest of the day off. If you need me just call. If you need help with something let me know and I will talk you through it if I have to," I told them before walking out of the building.

I hopped in my car not really knowing where I was fucking going until I got there. I was in a daze, but the anger was still there. I felt betrayed by the two bitches that I loved with all my heart. How could they both do some shit like this to me? I tried to calm myself down but there wasn't anything that I could do to make this pain go away.

I pulled up at my house twenty minutes later and parked right beside my sister's car. I already knew some fucked-up shit was going down because never was my sister home this early in the day.

I reached into my glove department and loaded my gun. I stepped out my car not really thinking at all. All I knew was that I wanted them both to pay for hurting me.

I understood that I had done a lot of shit to hurt Promise, but not once had I ever fucked with any of her family members. There was no way in hell I would have done some heartless shit like she had done.

A thought came across my mind, it said to get back in my car and just leave all of this shit alone, but the thought was just a thought. Revenge was so much better and sweeter. I opened the door and headed into the house with the gun clenched tightly in my hand.

I called out to Promise and Layla just to see where in the house they were at. They both called out that they were upstairs. As I walked up each step and as I got closer to the two people who had hurt me to my very core, that's when all the hate began to flood my heart. There wasn't going back now, not even if I wanted to.

I pushed open the door and pointed my weapon at them both.

Layla and Promise both screamed when they saw that I was aiming the weapon at them.

"You thought that I wasn't going to find out about yall fucking. Did yall really think yall was going to get away with this shit?"

Layla tried to deny it, but she quickly closed her mouth when I gave her the death stare.

"What's so hurtful is that you going to sit here and lie to me about ya'll not fucking when this room smells like pussy," I yelled out.

Layla began to cry but I ignored it.

"Someone took a picture of ya'll kissing at the hospital. I saw the shit with my own eyes. You can't fucking lie to me about any of this shit. Promise I've loved your ass through the good times and the bad.

Even though I have done a lot of shit I'm not proud of, never have I ever went behind your back and did some fucked up shit like you have done to me. Bitch, I went broke for your ass to make your dream come true as being a business owner. I have taken care of your ass since you first became my bitch, you never had to stress or worry about shit. Yes, I might have fucked a few bitches along the way, but no bitch compared to you, and not once did I ever leave you for any of them hoes. I thought we were better than this shit, but I guess I was wrong. You have taken this shit way to far when you involved my damn sister."

Promise began to cry but I ignored her ass and began to focus my attention towards my sister.

"Layla you my fucking sister, you know better. I have always been there for you when you needed me. If I knew you were going to move in and fuck my bitch behind my back I would have let your ass stayed with Bryson and continued to let him abuse you!" I screamed loudly.

"Please just let us explain," Promise cried.

"What the fuck do you need to explain bitch?" I asked her furiously.

"Last time I checked both of ya'll was strictly dickly, now all of sudden ya'll licking each other's pussy and shit."

I was beyond angry and was ready to blast both of their asses.

When Promise and Layla looked over at one another and grabbed each other's hand, that's when I took the time to take my gun off safety.

"Lamar, please put the gun down and let's talk about this like adults," Layla begged

"I don't want to talk about shit!" I screamed violently.

"Please don't do this," Promise begged.

"Don't beg now bitch!" I shouted before aiming the gun to Promise's head.

Just as I pulled the trigger that's when my baby sister jumped in front of Promise to save her from the first bullet.

Pow.

Layla hit the floor with a bullet to her chest. Blood spilled from her body, but I didn't give two fucks. Promise dropped down to the floor and held Layla in her arms as she screamed and cried.

"I love you," Promise cried out to my sister.

Layla tried speaking but blood fell from out her mouth as if it was a fountain. A few seconds later my sister took her last breath.

I walked over to where Promise was kneeling on the ground and didn't think twice about pulling the trigger yet again.

Blood and brain matter splattered over me.

Tears filled my eyes as I stood there and looked at the two females who I had once loved. Blood filled the hardwood floors and covered my shoes, face, and some parts of my shirt and pants. I walked over to the bed in a daze and sat down.

My tears blurred my vision of the bloody mess that laid a few feet away. My thoughts were so fucked up in my head that I couldn't think straight at the moment. All I knew was, I was going to go to prison for the rest of my life.

Did I really want that shit to go down like that? I asked myself.

I didn't see my life worth living any longer. My sister and my girl were all I had left. I didn't have anyone or anything that I wanted to live for. I was better off dead at least that was what I felt.

I could hear the police sirens in the distance and that's when it dawned on me that someone must have called the police about the shots being fired. I stared down at my pistol as I debated what to do next. A few seconds my decision was made when I heard the police pull up in my driveway.

I didn't hesitate to place the gun to my temple and squeeze the trigger.

Pow.

THE END.

CONNECT WITH ME ON SOCIAL MEDIA

- Subscribe to my mailing list by visiting my website: https://www.shaniceb.com/

- Like my Facebook author page: https://www.facebook.com/ShaniceBTheAuthor/?ref=aymt_homepage_panel

- Join my reader's group on Facebook. I post short stories and sneak peeks of my upcoming novels that I'm working on! https://www.facebook.com/groups/1551748061561216/

- Send me a friend request on Facebook: https://www.facebook.com/profile.php?Id=100011411930304&__nodl

- Follow me on Instagram: https://www.instagram.com/shaniceb24/?hl=en

ABOUT THE AUTHOR

Shanice B was born and raised in Georgia. At the age of nine years old, she discovered her love for reading and writing. At the age of ten, she wrote her first short story and read it in front of her classmates, who fell in love with her wild imagination. After graduating high school, Shanice decided to pursue her career in Early Childhood Education. After giving birth to her son, Shanice decided it was time to pick up her pen and get back to what she loved the most.

She is the author of over twenty books and is widely known for her bestselling four-part series titled Who's Between the Sheets: Married to A Cheater. Shanice is also the author of the three-part series, Love Me If You Can, and three standalones titled Stacking It Deep: Married to My Paper, A Love So Deep: Nobody Else Above you, and Love, I Thought You Had My Back. In November of 2016, Shanice decided to try her hand at writing a two-part street lit series titled Loving My Mr. Wrong: A Street Love Affair. Shanice resides in Georgia with her family and her five-year-old son.

<u>*NOW AVAILABLE ON AMAZON*</u>

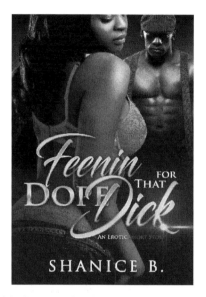

QUICK NOTE: This is a twelve-thousand-word erotic short story. If you are looking for something sexy and quick to read, then this will be the perfect read for you.

Heartbroken over her ex leaving her for another woman, Kira seems to not be able to shake her bruised ego. When Kira's best friend Shonda persuades her to have a girl's night out to take her mind off her heartbreak, Kira's life will forever be changed.

In walks Jacolby…

When Kira and Jacolby lock eyes on each other their burning desire and lust for one another is what they feel. Kira is FEENIN' for some dope dick and Jacolby just happens to be the man who is eager to please her inside and outside of the bedroom.

Once Jacolby dicks her down, Kira finds herself falling for him hard and fast and there is nothing she can do about it but let it happen.

When Kira's ex magically reappears, she must make a decision. Will she go back to the man that has broken her heart or will she remain with the one man who has swept her off her feet and made her feel things she has never felt before?

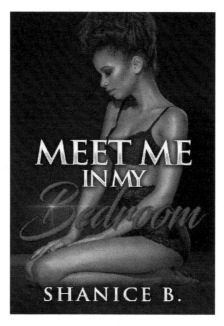

Meet Me In My Bedroom will have you glued to your kindle from the very first page.

These erotic love stories are steamy hot reads that are centered around romantic relationships.

Each love story is jaw dropping and will have you begging for more.

Read at your own risk. Enjoy!

Made in the USA
San Bernardino, CA
28 January 2020